Once Bitten, Twice Shy

Teresa J. Reasor

Contact Information: teresareasor@msn.com

Cover Art by Tracy Stewart
Edited by Faith Freewoman

Teresa J. Reasor
PO Box 124
Corbin, KY 40702

First Edition Published by Amazon as part of the Magic And Mayhem Kindleworld 6/17/2017

Publishing History: Second Edition 2018
ISBN 13: 978-1-940047-27-0
Print Edition

Table of Contents

Somewhere off the beaten path in the World of Magic and Mayhem, there's a little-visited trail that leads to a realm of vampire politics, danger and maybe even death.

Phoebe Stewart only agreed to marry Trevor Ricci to secure peace between their warring vampire clans. When her groom poisons her during the wedding ceremony, and her life expectancy falls from forever to a week, "till death do you part" takes on a whole new meaning. When she catches up with her new husband, she intends to stake and roast the traitorous, narcissistic weenie.

Especially now she's met Hunter Knox, the bad boy alpha vampire she's been waiting for her whole death.

Agent Hunter Knox works for the National Vampire Security Council. When a poison that can actually kill their species surfaces, he's dead set on finding and destroying it. But once he meets Phoebe, and realizes she only has days to live, the need for an antidote takes priority.

And the more he gets to know her, the more he suspects she may be as important to vampire kind as she's becoming to him.

Chapter 1

Friday, June 13th
Scryville, Kentucky

W*EDDINGS SUCK.*
Vampire weddings blow.

Phoebe sighed and folded her arms atop the gallery railing to peer down at the crowd.

The long line of guests stretched through the main entrance foyer and out the back door like a huge, deadly serpent.

Trevor, her groom, crossed the foyer, shook hands with someone in line, and spoke to them. Should she concentrate hard enough to eavesdrop on their conversation? Trevor moved on down the line, making the impulse moot.

The groom was handsome. If she'd met him in a club or during a function, he might have appealed to her...at least until he opened his mouth. His black hair gleamed in the soft light of the enormous chandelier hanging from the vaulted ceiling. His sky-blue eyes, strong jaw, and perfect mouth were easy on the eyes. His pale skin glowed, and even appeared to have a little color if she saw him soon after he fed. Yes, his looks were a definite lure, but after their first evening together, she recognized him for the narcissistic weenie he was.

When he smiled with just the right amount of lip, he could pass for human, something which might come in handy during business meetings with non-vampire species, but only made him seem manipulative to her.

Which was what this wedding represented. A high-level, well-attended business meeting to seal the deal on a crucial merger. And it was also what turned her off about him as soon as they met. The merger, and his calculated, manipulative charm.

What self-respecting vampire allowed themselves to be sold off as fast as a marked down Gucci handbag. Or was that thought a product of her long-dead human side sitting up and screaming in protest? After all, hadn't she allowed herself to be put into the same position?

Because she had to obey her sire. Whatever he needed of her, she was forced to agree to. But she had expected more consideration from Arthur. She tried to set aside the hurt, but it still knotted like a fist in the pit of her stomach.

However, dwelling on it would not change anything.

She shifted her attention to other concerns. Like what the hell they were supposed to do with the nine hundred wedding gifts. Was she expected to write nine hundred thank-you notes? That was so *not happening*!

As soon as Trevor disappeared into the study, Phoebe

strode across the gallery and down the hall to her suite.

The reasons behind the marriage were as medieval as the suit of armor in her sire's study. The bonding of two master vampires' territories through the marriage of their...for lack of a better word...children, smacked of the medieval as well.

The pomp and circumstance surrounding the whole thing was tiresome in the extreme. Why couldn't they go to Vegas, simply do the deed, and get it behind them? But other vampires seemed to enjoy these rare social occasions, where the conversations sounded like veiled threats, and the likelihood of violence was balanced on a razor's edge.

She'd only been to two weddings in her fifty-seven years as a vampire. This one was the second. And the first hadn't ended well for her either, since one of the groomsmen, one of her sire's minions, was responsible for her current condition, and the exclusively liquid diet it required.

And she was still pissed about it.

Today she craved a cheeseburger so badly she wanted to rip someone's head off. Even after all this time, she could still taste the delicious combination of beef, melted cheese, grilled onions, fresh tomato, and pickles. Her salivary glands kicked in, and she swallowed.

She'd tried eating one right after her transition. It had not ended well. She shuddered at the memory. Her undead system was as slow as a snake's, and insisted on a liquid diet she could absorb at her leisure. And, contrary to popular myth, a small meal every other week sufficed to sustain her. Maybe not as well as her sire would like, but well enough for her to bench-press a car if she needed to.

She did get to look twenty forever, though. There was always a trade-off, wasn't there? Which brought her straight back to the issue at hand.

This farce of a wedding.

She glanced at the clock and estimated how much time she had until she would be forced to make an appearance.

Her bedroom was decorated in cream and gold. She liked light—craved it—and since she didn't get to hang out in daylight anymore, she had to get her fix where she could. Crossing to the one large chair positioned facing the far bedroom wall, she sat down to concentrate on the three bold, beautiful images of the southeastern Kentucky mountains, the last photos she took before becoming a vampire. Blown up to poster size, they took up much of the empty wall space, and allowed her to enjoy sunlight in the only way open to her. And the illusion of sunlight allowed her to meditate, which calmed the wild nerves twisting her stomach into knots and kicking her usually slow-beating heart into a frenzy.

Finally, she heard the knock she'd been expecting. "Come in, Arthur."

He walked in, frowning. "Phoebe why are you not dressed?"

Arthur Stewart had become a vampire at age thirty, in

the 1200s. Though he'd lived in America since the Revolutionary War, he still spoke with a hint of a Scottish accent. His russet hair flowed back off his forehead, thick and healthy, and his pale skin still retained some color from the scattering of freckles across his cheekbones. Dressed in a dark Armani tux with a bow tie, he looked quite dashing.

"I still have time, Arthur. How long does it take to put on a dress and brush my hair?"

"Why is there no one here with you to help you prepare?"

Because their thrilled babble had been driving her crazy, and it was extremely important for her to remain calm. "I sent them away. I've been dressing myself since I was three. I think I can handle it."

Arthur lifted the small chair before the dressing table, set it in front of her, and sat, leaning forward to brace his elbows on his knees.

"Your life will not change as much as you think, Phoebe."

She remained silent while she studied the pictures over Arthur's shoulder. *It isn't going to change at all.*

"Do you not find Trevor handsome?"

She fought the urge to roll her eyes. "He knows he is."

Arthur's lips twitched suspiciously. "Charming?"

"Not particularly."

His brows rose at that. "What do you mean?"

"Don't try to put a positive spin on things, Arthur.

You've talked to the man. He's manipulative and slick. It's a game to him to see how easily he can charm someone, then once he's done so, he gets bored and moves on to the next challenge. He has no empathy for, or interest in anyone, but himself."

"But he is interested in you."

"Yes, the same way an entomologist is interested in a bug." But only because she wasn't impressed by Trevor. A new experience for him, she was sure.

There was a notch carved between Arthur's brows as he said, "So you feel nothing for him? No attraction at all?"

"No, I don't. It takes more than a pretty package." For the first time she felt distrustful of her sire's motivations. And wary.

She'd observed how Trevor treated the servants when he thought there were no witnesses. There was a cruel streak in him, as there was in all vampires. Including herself, when she needed there to be. But he enjoyed being cruel only to those he knew were weaker.

She suppressed the small twinge of fear. Since Trevor was older and physically stronger, he could easily hurt her if he wanted to. And if they were together long, he would eventually. And if she lost control, she would kill him.

To prevent the temptation, she had already arranged to leave as soon as the "I do's" were spoken. Arthur clearly no longer needed her input with his business interests. Otherwise he wouldn't have asked her to wed this male. And since he was cutting her loose, she could travel or do whatever else she pleased. She'd have time to finish her house in the mountains, and practice her photography once again.

She tried for the thousandth time to feel some excitement about being on her own with the freedom to do whatever she wished. But it was hard to feel excited when her heart was broken.

"What do you expect of him, Phoebe?"

"Nothing. You and Armanno are getting what you want, an end to the violence between his people and yours. Trevor is getting what he wants, control of part of his father's territory. All three of you can be satisfied."

"I had hoped to give you a partner to share things with, and who might possibly bring you happiness. It has been a long time since your last sojourn into romance."

She leaned back into her chair and struggled to maintain her relaxed pose in spite of the rage sizzling under every inch of her skin. "This is not the twelve hundreds, Arthur. Twenty-first century women"—she continued despite his raised brow—"do not need a mate to be happy. We make our own happiness. Since vampire women can't have children, what do any of us need a man for, anyway?" She needed a boy toy, or at least a vibrator with just the right settings. Trevor would never fulfill either desire.

"Why did you agree to this marriage if you don't expect to receive anything from it?"

She studied his handsome face. "I didn't know I had a choice."

"Phoebe..." he sighed her name. "In light of your nearly sixty years of loyalty, I might have given you a choice, had you asked."

Surprise and anger tumbled inside her. "Damn fine time to say so, Arthur, now it's far too late to back out."

His expression settled into a concerned frown. "Your position in Trevor's household will serve as a deterrent to violence. You know the recent deaths in Texas and Louisiana have unbalanced the powers in the south. Trevor knows if you are not well cared for, open war might erupt, which would not be good for humans, vampires, or any other species."

Trevor's household? She hadn't planned to stay in a household with "I'm so beautiful I have to check myself out in every mirror I pass" Trevor. She'd be alone in enemy territory.

"It's a given that they'll try to kill me, Arthur. They might well have heard rumors." Why had Arthur so easily given away his secret weapon? She used to believe she was a valued member of his clan. Why had he discarded her so easily?

Unless he hoped to achieve more than peace. Perhaps gain control of the entire southeastern part of the country. And why would he want it? It was headache enough to maintain control of the vampires in Scryville and the outlying counties.

"You will be providing a valued service to your clan,

Phoebe. We need someone who will keep a close eye on both Ricci and Trevor. And you'll have bodyguards living with you. Not that you really need them."

But it was not he who would have to put up with Trevor. "I really believed this marriage thing was going to be a symbolic gesture, not a real deal. You don't actually expect me to be a real wife to him, do you?"

He got to his feet, suddenly very eager to leave. "What the two of you make of this...situation is up to you. But you may want to have a conversation with Trevor at your earliest convenience." He whipped out the door with vampiric speed.

Her cheeks flared with heat and she leapt to her feet, almost following him, but what good would it do? They had over a thousand guests outside, strolling beneath the stars, listening to music, and filling their glasses at the blood fountain. There was no time for a heart-to-heart with Trevor. Damn him, and damn Arthur as well.

The urge to leave her groom standing alone at the altar spun through her thoughts. It would be an insult to Ricci and Trevor, and an embarrassment to her sire. Everyone would expect Arthur to punish her for the slight. Vampire punishments could be anything from a staking to slow torture, and she preferred to avoid pain whenever possible.

She struggled to keep from shrieking in frustration and bared her fangs instead.

"Shit!"

Chapter 2

S HE'D CHOSEN A jade green floor-length gown with a sweetheart bodice and cap sleeves to wear for the wedding ceremony. But that was before Arthur's enlightening conversation.

To replace the gown, she made a quick run to a nearby store and chose a leather bustier that pushed her generous breasts up and flashed more bare skin than she was used to. But, hey! A girl only got married once.

Leather pants hugged her hips and thighs, and knee-high boots with spiked heels added four inches to her height, making her five eight. Instead of a bouquet, she carried a riding crop. She loved the way it sounded when she whipped it through the air.

She'd like it even better if she could use it to beat some sense into Arthur.

She pulled her hair back off her face and French braided it down the back. It was better to have one's hair secured out of the way when intending to bite someone. Kept the blood from making it stiff.

She also played up her makeup. She might not wear it

often, but she knew how to apply it skillfully when she needed to.

Arthur's eyes widened when she appeared, but he quickly assumed an entirely blank face when she sauntered up to him.

"You look very natural in leather, my dear. You should wear it more often."

The strains of a classical guitar playing Pachelbel's *Canon in D* drifted through the French doors and into the hall. She looped her hand through Arthur's arm while firmly suppressing the desire to rip it off and beat him to death with it.

"Just so you know, Arthur, I know when I'm being played. And I don't appreciate it." She couldn't entirely conceal the bitterness in her voice. "I expected better of you."

The scent of burning candles was strong as they stepped out onto the long concrete patio, but didn't overwhelm the perfume of the flowers decorating the buffet tables and the huge urns on either side of the steps.

Arthur shot her a cautioning look. "I don't know what you mean, Phoebe."

"Hah!"

Arthur's mouth twitched. "If you are ready, my dear."

She thrust her chin up and ground her teeth. "'Let the wild rumpus start.'" She couldn't wait to get this over with and be on her way.

Chairs were arranged in a huge semicircle, divided by a long aisle down the center. Trevor's sire, Armanno Ricci, and the rest of his entourage and guests, sat on the right, while Arthur's sat on the left.

Phoebe often read the phrase, "Silence is louder than words," but she had never truly believed it until she started down the aisle to join the two tall males on the platform framed by an arbor woven with black roses.

To cover her nerves, she used a little more hip action while she walked, and tapped the riding crop in a measured beat against her thigh.

A chill had hit the mountains just after dusk, and though she rarely reacted to changes in temperature, she was glad for the leather sheathing her body.

When they arrived at the dais, Arthur held her hand while she climbed the steps. With a bow, he stepped back and took a seat in the front row.

Phoebe offered Trevor a smile that was all fang. He eyed her warily as she took her place next to him. Was her rage apparent? She hoped so.

"Just so you know," she murmured into his ear. "I always like to be on top, and I enjoy inflicting pain." She tapped his behind with the crop hard enough to give him a little sting. He jerked.

"I hope you like being spanked, Trevor."

His eyes widened in surprise, then narrowed in distaste.

She fought down a gleeful grin. "I wouldn't want to be

accused of misrepresentation later."

Harry Adcock, their master of ceremonies—he wasn't a minister—looked down his blade-thin nose and narrowed his beady eyes. Tall, skinny, and wearing Vampire Council robes, he looked like a crow. Sparse hair swept over his balding head in a failed comb-over. He released a warning flow of power, glared at her, and then cleared his throat. "Shall we begin?"

Phoebe smiled back. "I'm ready when you are, Councilman Ad-cock." She allowed a hint of her power to escape and wash over the two men. Both males stiffened as though she'd farted. Trevor eased away from her about a foot.

She'd been told her power caused a pain/pleasure sensation not everyone enjoyed. Hopefully, by the time the evening was over, Trevor would want to be farther away than just a foot. Perhaps more like the width of the state. She was going to make it her lifelong ambition to encourage maximum distance between them.

Phoebe listened to what Adcock was saying with only half an ear while she scanned the crowd for trouble. Armanno Ricci was scowling, and his dark eyes homed in on her. She met his eyes for a moment. His eyebrows rose when his power had no effect on her.

Adcock reached the dreaded vows stage of the ceremony, and Phoebe dragged her attention back to him and Trevor.

"Do you, Phoebe, take Trevor as your mate, to honor,

14

protect, and obey?"

"Obey? O-bey?" She raised her eyebrows and tilted her head. "Not going to happen, Adcock. Wishful thinking."

He paused with his mouth open.

"A. Deal. Breaker." She emphasized each word.

"I agree to having that part of the vows taken out of the ceremony," Trevor said. Was that an actual blush tinging his skin?

"Thank you, Trevor. Dear." Though she knew it wasn't in the ceremony, she added, "When it comes to your vows of obedience, I'll do the same."

Adcock inhaled, and his nostrils narrowed further. If he kept doing it, they were going to collapse.

"Do you, Phoebe, agree to honor and protect Trevor, for as long as you both shall live?"

An eternity to be responsible for a stranger. Phoebe glanced over at Arthur. She didn't want to claim the man standing next to her. Everything inside her was screaming for her to walk away. Arthur nodded, and her stomach fell. Tears stung her eyes and she looked away. The congregation behind her had begun to shift in their seats before she managed a resentful, "I do."

"Do you, Trevor, agree to honor and protect Phoebe, for as long as you both shall live?"

His "I do" was louder, and held a hard note of triumph, as did the dark glow in his eyes when he looked at her.

"The ceremony will conclude with the sharing of blood

between husband and wife," Adcock announced.

Nausea hit Phoebe. She held out her wrist.

"I prefer your neck, Phoebe."

He could deliberately hurt her for embarrassing him before his people. No one would stop him. She turned her chin and exposed the soft side of her throat.

He smelled of spicy cologne and something like cloves or evergreen as he tilted her jaw just a little and delicately struck her neck with his fangs. It didn't seem he drank at all, but just rubbed his lips against her throat in a kiss. He wiped a thumb across the puncture wounds. His mouth was barely red with her blood when he stepped back, wiping it away with a handkerchief. There was an unwanted intimacy about his unfastening his tie and unbuttoning his shirt to expose his neck. He held aside his collar and presented his throat.

She hadn't bitten a live source of blood in a long time. Also, she hadn't eaten in nearly two weeks. Bad idea. The strong beat of Trevor's pulse thrummed against his skin. He had obviously eaten before the ceremony.

Phoebe homed in on his heartbeat, saliva pooled in her mouth, and her fangs dropped. She bit him delicately, tasting the salty sweetness of his blood...and something else.

Her lips and tongue went numb, and her throat tightened. Her neck where he'd bitten her began to burn. She staggered back. Then her legs gave out and she landed hard on her hip.

What was happening?

Poison, it had to be some kind of poison. But how had he dosed her? Not his blood, his skin. Maybe his mouth, where he had bitten her? "Yu sn o bith!"

"Did you really think I'd agree to marry a cold bitch who doesn't know her place, Phoebe? Did you think I wouldn't know how powerful you are?" He eyed her with disgust.

He reached over and broke off a piece of the wooden arbor. He was going to stake her. Helpless, she braced herself, while she frantically looked around for help.

She looked to Adcock. His beady eyes darted between her and Trevor's broad shoulders before he dashed off the platform toward the heavy stand of trees at the end of the yard.

Bedlam erupted as vampires on both sides leapt to their feet and turned on each other. Roars and hisses were followed by a several crashes when chairs were flung or crushed as the crowd clashed in hand-to-hand combat.

A male vampire rushed up on the platform and pounced on Trevor, shoving him away from her. The two struggled, their teeth bared, fighting for control of the stake. Trevor twisted the young male's arm, snapping it, and swung him toward Phoebe. Her would-be rescuer tripped over her and tumbled away.

Trevor leaped off the platform and advanced toward Arthur, her sire. If he killed Arthur, every vampire in his line would go down, including her. With one strike, an entire clan would be murdered. But if she took out his sire first...

Phoebe shook her head to clear her vision.

The clamor around her faded into the background while she focused on the lit candles on either side of the arbor. She stretched out a hand, letting loose the witchy part of her that had survived her transition. Heat rushed over her, making the leather pants and bustier feel tight. As though through the bottom of a bottle, she saw the fire, a dull light, and called it to her. The flame leaned toward her.

The candle dropped off its holder and she caught it. The fire stung her skin momentarily before it built into a ball of flame cupped in her palm. She drew its power into her, holding the fire inside and projecting it outward. Her limbs wouldn't obey her when she tried to get to her feet, so she rolled on the wooden platform, fighting against Trevor's toxin.

She couldn't throw the fire, but she could roll it. She slung the flame along the floor, and it sped toward Trevor's dark-haired sire, Armanno Ricci. His legion of men surrounded him. One vampire ran forward and stomped at the fire, but it dodged his feet and looped around him, climbing his leg and setting his suit on fire. He screamed and twisted, batting frantically at his clothing, while the other vamps scattered.

For a time she lost control of the flame and, like a thing possessed, it leapt from vampire to vampire, setting their hair and clothing on fire, burning their faces off, growing larger with every vampire it consumed. She struggled to contain it, to pull it back, but she was getting weaker by the moment.

Her body shook while she gathered it. Like a tornado of flame, it speared into the sky, then lanced downward, stabbing into the heart of the Ricci clan, and pointing like a finger at Armanno Ricci. She held it poised over him.

Armanno screamed, staggered back, and fell, throwing up an arm to protect himself. His small legion of vampires froze, the threat of his death holding them in thrall. They would all fall should he burn.

Arthur stepped through the throng. His shirt was ripped, and his hair mussed, but he remained in one piece. "You will heal my daughter, Armanno. Otherwise, you and your people will all die. Especially that ball-less ass you call a son." Arthur pointed at Trevor, who was being held by three of his men.

The Ricci sire slithered out from under the finger of fire, and reaching into his pocket, removed a vial. "It is the antidote. And you must hurry! Otherwise, she will not survive." He tossed the glass tube.

Arthur caught it in midair and rushed to Phoebe's side. Phoebe shook her head. What if it was a trick and she ingested more poison instead of a cure? Sound reached her as though she heard each word through a layer of cotton.

"He's telling the truth, Phoebe," Arthur urged. "You must release the blaze."

She rolled onto her back and opened her fisted hands.

The fire collapsed into itself and disappeared. Her vision blurred, then went dark while her head swam. Arthur raised her to a sitting position, cracked open the vial of clear fluid, and emptied it into her mouth.

The bitter taste coated her tongue, beating back the numbness. Arthur rubbed her throat as though that would help her swallow the fluid. Blackness closed around her, and she died.

Chapter 3

ROGER HAINES, VAMPIRE investigator for Have Wand, Will Travel, eyed him across the desk. Roger's face, lit by the glow of a small lamp, appeared to be all hollows and angles. Vampires weren't supposed to lose weight or change in any great way after their transition, but damned if ol' Roger didn't look overworked and undernourished.

Roger dove directly into why he'd called Hunter. "Hunter, I've been asked by the Vampire Council to investigate what happened at the wedding of Trevor Ricci and Phoebe Stewart. Seventeen of Armanno Ricci's clan were burned to dust in a matter of moments. And Council member Harry Adcock is making some pretty wild accusations."

Hunter raised a brow. "And you're telling me this because...?"

"Some of the stuff he's saying is...out there, Hunter. He's making accusations against Phoebe and Arthur Stewart, saying it was an ambush."

"Based on what I've heard, there's a question of who ambushed who."

"So you know about it?" Roger seemed relieved.

"One of our staff looked into it. I only know what was said around the blood cooler."

Roger leaned forward in his seat and rested his elbows on the desk. "Which was?"

"Trevor Ricci, the groom, attempted a coup. He married Phoebe, the adopted daughter of Arthur Stewart, then attempted to kill her when they exchanged blood bites. She nearly died on the platform. A fight broke out, and one of the members of Ricci's party caught fire during the struggle. It seems there were candles everywhere. In the throes of his burning, it spread to several other members of Ricci's party."

"Adcock insists that Phoebe had a fire-throwing device."

"While she was lying on the platform, dying, she was also throwing fire?"

"It's what he's alleging." Roger paused and rose to his feet. "She's in the room next door, waiting to see you."

"To see me? Why?"

"Look, Hunter. I'm overwhelmed here. I have so many cases I don't have time to deal with this one. And it's a conflict of interest for me to work for both her and the Vampire Council at the same time on the same case. I've already told her I'm passing it off to a different agent, saying you work for another PI agency. I think she's gotten a raw deal, and she needs your help."

"How so?"

His thin face tautened, and his mouth compressed.

"She's dying. The antidote for the poison was only a temporary fix. Trevor was being held to stand trial before the Council, but he's escaped. If you don't find him, retrieve the poison, and get it to our human scientists so they can find a real antidote, she'll die—permanently."

"Shit!" He didn't know this female vampire, but his outrage and concern kicked in anyway.

Roger stood and moved around his desk. "Her poisoning is proof of attempted murder, and it could be a threat to others. We both know how hard we are to kill. If this should kill her, it would prove he's in possession of something so deadly it could wipe out any number of our kind. That alone should give you sufficient reason to pursue this."

Hunter remained silent for a moment. "You haven't told her who I work for?"

"No. She thinks you're on loan from another private detective agency."

He nodded. "Okay. I'll meet with her."

Roger grinned and nodded. "Come with me, and I'll introduce you."

Hunter followed Roger down the hall to another office. A woman was standing at the window, her back to the room, but she turned to face them as soon as Roger spoke. Her skin glowed pale and flawless. Her large violet eyes tracked Hunter as he crossed to the desk and came to a standstill.

There was an elfin quality in the width of her cheekbones and the point of her chin. Her hair was a blend of different shades of blond, but had been streaked with dark mahogany. She wore a short leather jacket, a turtleneck sweater, jeans, and boots.

She walked toward the desk with the preternatural grace of the vampire she was, but there were shadows beneath her eyes, and just above the edge of the turtleneck a purplish-black bruise discolored the skin.

She stopped across the desk from Hunter and nodded.

Roger made the introductions. "This is Hunter Knox, Ms. Stewart. I trust he'll give your case his full attention. He's agreed that, as long as he's on the case, he'll have no other clients but you."

That wasn't quite true, unless Hunter's bosses at the National Vampire Security Council decided this was as important as he thought they would. His report would make the poison the center of the investigation, though saving Ms. Stewart's life would certainly take precedence too.

"Thank you, Mr. Haines."

The hoarse, raspy sound of her voice surprised Hunter. Was that an aftereffect of the poison, or her normal voice? He wondered what her laughter sounded like.

"I'll leave you two to talk." Roger bowed his way out and closed the door.

"You can call me Hunter, Ms. Stewart." He offered his hand across the desk. She returned his handshake with a businesslike pressure. As Stewart's daughter, she'd be used to dealing with men.

Hunter moved to take a seat in one of the clients' chairs, leaving the desk chair to her. She lowered herself into the seat very carefully.

They stared at each other for several moments. At once aware of her simmering power, his pulse picked up. He had met vampires with special abilities before. Though she attempted to hide it, her control was slipping, undoubtedly because of her illness.

"How are you feeling?"

"I've been better." She reached for a plastic cup with a straw in it and drank deeply. He smelled fresh blood.

"I'd rather hear about how the poison has affected you. We need to document everything, so when we find your fiancé, appropriate measures can be taken to punish him." He grabbed a legal pad and pen.

She hesitated for a moment, fidgeting. "The bite burns incessantly. Trevor bit me, then rubbed poison into the wounds with his thumb. I feel dizzy when I move too quickly. My body is wearing itself out trying to heal, so I must feed often." She lifted the cup in demonstration. "My physician has told me when my body can no longer keep up with the demands of the poison, I'll die."

Hunter swallowed to moisten his suddenly dry mouth. Her death would be a damn shame. He didn't know what her gifts were, but every diverse member of their species brought something valuable to the clans.

"Tell me about your—fiancé." He was strangely reluctant to call the man her husband.

"I underestimated him. I thought he was just a self-absorbed weenie, but instead he was a treacherous, murderous asshole."

She had a right to be angry, but it wouldn't help Hunter build a case. "Tell me about him, where he might go, what he might do, now he's on the run from his clan and most other vamps."

"I don't really know him. We only met twenty-four hours before the ceremony. I'm not old enough to rise early during the day, so we only spoke for about two hours the night before the wedding. He and his sire Armanno Ricci and Arthur spent most of the night in the library hammering out some last-minute changes to the contract." She shot him a wry smile. "It was supposed to quell the violence between our clans."

"I see. How did you feel about the marriage?"

She remained silent for several moments. "Arthur is my sire, and he was doing what he thought best for our clan."

Meaning she hadn't been happy with the arrangement, but she wasn't going to say anything negative about her sire. But he sensed pain behind the care she took choosing her words.

"And Trevor? How did he seem?"

"He was gaining control of a third of his sire's territory. I thought he was pleased with the deal."

"What can you tell me about him?"

"He looks thirty. He's fifty years older than I am, which makes him about a hundred. He spoke of finishing his degree long after his transition so he could help Ricci with his business interests. They've been together since before he was turned. He can ride horseback. Likes to go for moonlight swims."

Hunter raised a brow at that.

Phoebe grinned as though sharing a joke, and for a moment he saw the vibrant young vampire behind the illness. And she was very, very ill.

She sipped more blood before setting the cup aside. "He thought I'd find it romantic. He also mentioned some friends. I met one of them. His name is Randal Hawkins. The other is Jack Kinney, who plays poker for a living."

"You learned all that in two hours?"

She shrugged. "He was eager to talk about himself and his friends. I'm a good listener when I feel I need to be. Also, I read Arthur's in-depth dossier on him."

"And you?"

"I wasn't interested in sharing. This was a business deal between my sire and his. It was never meant to be a real marriage. It was never going to be a marriage, as far as I was concerned. But Ricci and Trevor got greedy. With my death, they'll be one step closer to taking over the whole southeast territory.

"My clan won't sit back and wait. Violence will become

a way of life, and the whole area may explode, because the clan will think it's mandatory to seek vengeance for my death. Which means humans may be dragged into it. Other species."

"Unless your clan gets Ricci first."

"Arthur had a chance. He chose to save me instead. He has a sense of the big picture when others see only the wealth and power gained by being the leader of such a huge territory. He views wiping out an entire clan as genocide, and wants to avoid it if possible."

He'd never heard such a claim. "Forgive me, but I've never met an altruistic vampire. Most are solely involved in their own small corner of the world."

She shot him a narrow-eyed look. "Arthur is eight hundred years old. He's seen war, pestilence, and hardship. He wants what's best for our species. If we mean to survive, we need to learn to blend into the rest of society instead of hiding. Meet with him and let him tell you himself. But you might want to do so quickly." She struggled to her feet and gripped the edge of the desk.

Hunter rushed with vampiric speed to her side. He rested one hand against the small of her back while the other caught and held her arm to steady her. She smelled of orange blossoms. The feminine feel of her curves triggered an electric rush of awareness. She was smaller than he first thought, possibly only a hundred and fifteen pounds. The three-inch heels on her boots made her seem taller, but it couldn't add any bulk to her slender frame.

"I'm fine." She seemed more embarrassed than upset by the momentary weakness. She tilted her head back to look up at him, and their eyes locked.

Her unusual violet eyes darkened, then dropped away, her throat working as she swallowed. "I don't have time to waste. I've already started a search for Trevor myself, so if you're going to help me, you need to do it quickly."

She shifted away, and he released her.

"I'm aware of the time issue. And you said if. I thought the whole point of this interview was for me to work for you."

The distrust in her expression was open. "I don't know who you work for, Mr. Knox, but I know it's not just another private detective agency."

He canted his head in surprise. "Why do you say that?"

"You're wearing a three-thousand-dollar suit, and the Jaguar you drive is worth close to seventy thousand. I watched you pull up in it. You couldn't afford either one on a PI's salary."

She was no naïve, protected, adopted daughter of a wealthy Master Vampire. The shrewd suspicion in her gaze almost triggered a smile. "I'm independently wealthy, Ms. Stewart." Which wasn't a lie. "I do what I do because it's a challenge, and I enjoy helping people get the justice they deserve."

"The stakes for this investigation are higher than just

stolen property or a missing person."

"I'm aware of that."

"Mr. Haines is investigating what happened at the wedding for the local Vampire Council."

"I'm sure there's nothing to be worried about."

"I'm not worried. Harry Adcock is a fool and a coward. When the fighting broke out, the old buzzard ran and hid. As far as I'm concerned, he can take a flying leap onto a sharp stake, ass first."

"Since he's a member of the Vampire Council, you may want to be careful of what you say about him."

"If I live, *he* may want to be careful. I have video of him standing directly behind Trevor while he prepared to stake me. Adcock ran away even though he had an opportunity to help. He'd better think long and hard about this. If he pushes it, I'll release that video, and I'll own his position on the Council."

Hunter struggled between a sense of outrage on her behalf and amusement. Even ill, she had more passion and strength than Adcock, who was hundreds of years old. "I hope you've shared the video with Roger."

"Yes. I have. When would you like to speak with Arthur?"

"Tomorrow night, if possible."

"Do you have a card? I'll have him call you and set up a time."

"Certainly." He slipped a business card out of the inner

pocket of his suit jacket and handed it to her. It had nothing on it but his name and number. She tucked it into her jeans pocket and bent to retrieve a motorcycle helmet off the floor. She held it against her hip under her arm, and he stepped back to make room for her to slip out from behind the desk.

"May I see your neck?"

She tilted her head and tugged the turtleneck down, baring her throat. The fang marks hadn't healed, and the bruise covered an area from her jaw to her collarbone.

Concern pinched him. There was no substance he knew of that could cause such damage. If the flesh started rotting... She wouldn't be able to recover. Rage fired through him at the deliberate cruelty of what had been done. He fought the urge to draw her close.

"I thought Trevor was just wiping away the blood from his bite. He rubbed poison into the wound with his thumb. It will not heal."

He swallowed back his anger with difficulty while trying to keep his expression neutral. "Would you be open to having a physician I know examine you?"

Those violet eyes scanned his face again. "Yes."

"Good. I'll set it up right away." He was reluctant to let her go. Someone might be impatient for her to die and try to hurry things along out in the parking lot. "I'll see you out."

They walked down the hall to the waiting area. The PI agency's receptionist, Calamity, rose. As usual, her pale blonde hair tumbled around her shoulders in disarray, but she seemed well organized.

"It was good to see you again, Phoebe," she said. "Let me know if there's anything I can do."

Phoebe paused to give her a nod. "I appreciate the offer. Let me know the next time you do an evening youth seminar, and I'll help out."

The young witch's eyes glazed with tears for a moment before she regained control. "Thanks, I will."

His curiosity piqued, Hunter waited until they were outside to ask, "How do you know Calamity?"

"We became friends when I first transitioned. I didn't know it isn't really an accepted thing for a vampire to be friends with a witch. I thought we were all sort of in the same boat, being outside the realm of humankind." She gave a one-shouldered shrug. "Some of the younger witches have questions about vampires, and I help separate the truth from the myth. She does classes at the school to help them accept their powers and understand some of the other preternatural beings they may come in contact with. Prejudice is all about fear and ignorance."

"How long have you been one of us?"

"Fifty-seven years."

His brows rose. She had the poise and power of a much older vampire. Was it because of her gifts, or the strength of her personality? "I'll have more questions for you tomorrow. I don't want to tire you too much tonight. I'd like a copy of the dossier on Trevor Ricci, a list of the guests who attended the wedding, and the records of Stewart's upper management team when we meet."

Phoebe brushed back strands of the streaked mahogany hair which had fallen across her face. "Don't hold back, please. You need to push hard, because I may not have much time."

He fought the urge to comfort her. He was a stranger, and she didn't seem the type to welcome it. But he was drawn to her. He'd never before seen a vampire with violet eyes or with mahogany-streaked blond hair. Or one the Vampire Council could not intimidate.

"There are some other arrangements I have to make before I speak with Stewart and get his views on the bigger picture." He purposely used her description of the elder vampire. And it would give Hunter time to close out a couple of other cases and bring his boss up to speed on this development.

"I'll give him your card and ask him to call you right away."

She stepped down off the stairs, and he followed. She glanced back.

"I don't like the idea of you being out here alone."

The streetlight touched the blond in her hair with highlights, but cast her features in shadow. "I'm not alone." She signaled, and two large vampires emerged from the shadows of the doorways across the street. He hadn't even sensed them. He'd have to ask tomorrow how they'd masked their power. "There are two more behind you."

He twisted around to look behind him. They were each twenty or thirty feet away, but they were there. Large, powerfully built, and close enough to cover the distance in a matter of seconds, should he threaten her. He was either losing his edge, or there was something else going on here. He'd figure out what it was once he delved more deeply into the investigation and her.

"What time do you usually rise?" he asked.

"Nine. The one thing I find the most frustrating is sleeping so many hours. It's just so—boring."

"The older you are, the less you'll sleep." If she lived. "I'll be there before nine—Ms. Stewart." He barely caught himself before calling her Phoebe.

Her eyes caught the glow of the streetlight, and he sensed her wrestling with her emotions for a moment before she murmured, "Thank you."

He stood back, watching her put on her helmet and fasten the chinstrap. She threw up a hand, started the Harley Davidson street bike, knocked up the kickstand with her heel, and shot out of the parking lot like a bat out of hell. The other motorcycles fell in behind her, their roar like lions joining the hunt.

Hunter turned on his heel and retraced his steps to Roger's office. He tapped on the door and immediately heard an invitation to enter. "I need a copy of the wedding video

Phoebe gave you, a picture of her fiancé, and any information you've compiled on him. I'll get a list of the guests from her tomorrow."

Roger grinned. "I knew you'd take the job."

He had to maintain a professional distance, but it was going to be hard. She was beautiful and vulnerable right now. "I'm going after this asshole, and when I find him, after he's given up the poison, I'm going to see him staked. Whatever this is, it's deadly to us all."

Chapter 4

Phoebe entered the house and tossed her motorcycle keys into the sterling silver dish on the hall table. Something Hunter said had triggered a cascade of thoughts, one right after another. He believed someone here was involved. He wouldn't have asked for dossiers on the staff and business team otherwise…but who?

She paused to listen to the familiar ebb and flow of the house. Someone was in the kitchen, more than likely the housekeeper, Penelope, who was human. She loved her tea, and Phoebe heard the familiar sounds of the whistling teapot, and a spoon clanking against a cup.

"Good evening, Miss Phoebe."

Luke's Rhett Butler Georgia accent had a smile springing to her face, and she twisted around to face him. The room tilted, and she grabbed the edge of the table to save herself from hitting the floor.

Strong hands caught her arm and waist and held her steady. "Hey, take it easy, Phoebe."

She kept her eyes closed until the world quit spinning, and she felt it safe to open them. She tilted her head back to look up into Luke's thin, boyish face to see his blond curls had been shorn recently to a close cap against his head. He looked older with the new style. "When did you get back?"

He flashed her a smile. "Just a few hours ago. I was surprised you weren't here."

Usually she was an open book to him, but Arthur had cautioned her about sharing too much with anyone. "I had to get out for a while. Cabin fever was getting me down, so I took a ride on my motorcycle."

He frowned. "Not alone."

"No. The Hamiltons went with me."

"Good. They don't have much finesse, but they're deadly enough." He rested a hand on her shoulder. "How are you feeling?"

Like staked shit. "I'm fine. Just a little dizzy sometimes."

He pinched her chin, turned her head, and tugged the turtleneck away to look at her neck. "It doesn't look any worse."

But it wasn't getting any better. It throbbed like a heartbeat. She felt tired much of the time. And no matter how much blood she drank, it didn't heal.

She pulled away. "I'm tired of talking about it. I need to give Arthur a message right now, but then maybe we can go for a run."

He frowned. "Are you sure it's a good idea?"

"I'm not putting my life on hold because of this." She pointed at her throat. "I might as well light myself on fire if I do that. I need as much normal as possible."

"Okay. I get it. I'll go change and wait for you out by the patio."

"Thanks, Luke."

She waited until he had climbed the grand staircase to the second floor before she shrugged her leather jacket off, hung it in the hall closet, and rested back against the door.

What frightened her most was if her body became too weak to do any of the things she loved, because then she'd be trapped in her room. She'd be damned if she'd lie around so the servants and visitors could watch while she got weaker and weaker. To add even more horror to it, she could be on the brink of death for weeks. Her vampire constitution wouldn't stop trying to heal itself until there was nothing left to heal.

She wouldn't end her pain, because to commit suicide by sun went against every survival instinct in her vampire body. But mostly she wouldn't because it would give the Ricci clan what they wanted. Trevor would be second in line to control Stewart clan territory. Just as Trevor's death would offer her the same position in the Ricci clan. It was to be a stalemate situation to ensure one side had just as much to lose as the other. Should both of them die…

She brushed a weary hand over her forehead. If vampires could get headaches, the ramifications of this tangled mess would have given her one.

She'd suspected all along that Trevor was going to be a

pain in the ass. Had she known how big a hemorrhoid, she'd have staked him and gladly accepted her punishment.

She turned left and went down the hall to the library, tapping on the closed door.

Arthur opened the door himself. "Come in, Phoebe."

He shut the door and drew her to one of the two large leather couches facing each other in the center of the room. A large, square coffee table sat between them. "What did Roger say?"

"The Vampire Council has asked Roger to look into what happened at the wedding. They seem to be more concerned about the fire than they are about Trevor's attempted coup and the poison."

Arthur's expression remained unconcerned as he tugged at one sleeve of his sports coat. "That was to be expected, since Harry Adcock was there. He is beyond incompetent, and unable to see anything beyond the threat to his own useless neck."

She certainly agreed with that. "Roger passed my case onto someone else. His name is Hunter Knox."

Arthur leaned back against the soft leather. "What do you think of him?"

Her sire didn't need to hear how sexy she found him. Piercing gray eyes, dark brown hair, a chiseled jaw, a nose with just a little bit of a hook so his face wasn't too pretty, but handsome anyway, and a mouth she could spend hours just looking at, but would prefer to get much more intimately acquainted with. He had a deep voice, just hoarse enough to give her chills if he whispered in her ear. Being poisoned hadn't done a thing to her libido. Her heart started to race.

"He's at least two hundred years old, tall, intense. He seemed very focused. He wants to meet with us tomorrow evening." She pulled the card out of her jeans pocket and offered it to him. "I told him you'd call and arrange a time for him to come to the house."

"Very well."

"He wants another doctor to examine me."

"It can't hurt to get a second opinion," Arthur said. The hope she read in his face was hard to bear.

"I told him it would be fine. Maybe this doctor will be more up-to-date on things like this than Dr. Simons."

She was a realist. She knew how she felt. If they couldn't find Trevor within the week, she would have to make peace with her death.

"I'm sorry, Phoebe. I should have never placed you in such a position. I truly thought I was doing the right thing. Not just for us, but for all vampire kind."

She clamped off the quick rush of resentment and pain. "You weren't to know Trevor was so clever, Arthur. He had me fooled as well. But I really do wish you'd staked Ricci."

"To wipe out an entire bloodline would be genocide, Phoebe, and not something I can contemplate lightly. It would have killed twenty percent of Ricci's people, and left the clan in chaos."

Wouldn't that have been a good thing?

What did it say about her that she could so easily have made that choice? But it had been in the heat of battle. And in the end, she did call back the fire. "You wouldn't have had to stake him through the heart, just a knee or somewhere especially painful."

Arthur smiled broadly enough to show fang. "I could have done so, had he not flown off like the vulture he is. I was too concerned for you to follow and exact revenge."

Phoebe brushed an imaginary piece of lint off her sweater sleeve and fought back the threatened tears. "They would have expected you to do it, and might have tried to ambush you. It's good you didn't."

"I expected them to make some kind of move, Phoebe, but not this. You tried to warn me, and I didn't listen. I'm truly sorry."

"You weren't to know. I was on the lookout for trouble to come from Ricci's guests, not Trevor. I miscalculated, too."

She drew a deep breath, though she rarely needed one. "When the time comes, Arthur, I want my ashes scattered on the western side of mountain range. I've missed the sun on my face. I'll get it there."

"That isn't going to happen for a thousand years or more, my dear."

"Then you should have plenty of time to plan a very elaborate send-off for me. Like one of those New Orleans funerals with the jazz band and a parade. Or maybe everyone could celebrate Cinco De Mayo and paint their faces and hands like skeletons. That would be rather appropriate, don't you think?"

"May fifth has come and gone. You'll have to wait a thousand years, plus some months."

"I'm sure my ancestors won't mind if we fudge a month or two." She looked up at him. "You weren't disappointed in me for putting on such a spectacle at the wedding?"

"Never. You are my daughter, Phoebe. I am always proud of you."

Then why did you give me away so easily?

"You looked magnificent in leather with your riding crop. Your promise to spank the groom thrilled quite a few of males in the audience."

"I should have hit Trevor harder."

He chuckled. "We're going to find him, and exact revenge...after we get the poison and the antidote."

"What if he won't give up the formula, Arthur?"

"I will compel him. He is not strong enough to refuse either of us."

She nodded, not because she believed Arthur would succeed, but because she couldn't bear to be negative in the face of his optimism.

Sick of her pity party, she turned aside to brush the pinkish tears off her lashes. "Luke is waiting for me. I told him we'd go for a run together."

A flash of concern darted across his eyes. "I would prefer you stayed closer to the house, Phoebe. Perhaps a swim instead."

Her hand went to her throat. Would the chlorine in the water burn more than the injury itself?

"Okay. We can enjoy a swim and a movie. Though a movie isn't the same without hot, buttered popcorn," she complained.

"It's been almost sixty years since you've had that particular treat. How can you remember what it was like?"

"Any time you walk past a movie theater and smell it, it brings back the memory of how it tastes."

Arthur's features softened, and he brushed a kiss across her forehead. "Since I was born three hundred years before corn of any kind was imported to Britain, I have no memory of it."

"I'm sorry, Arthur." There were so many things he hadn't experienced before being reborn as a vampire.

"You can't miss something you never had, Phoebe."

She nodded. It still hurt her. But not as much as his betrayal.

"Go have your swim and watch your movie. I have some work that must be done, and I'll make the call to this Hunter Knox."

Chapter 5

THE FRAGRANCE OF peonies blooming against the side of the house hung sweet in the moist air.

Luke stood up when she joined him on the concrete steps, bowing his back, his body stretching, long and slim, but muscular—unsurprising, since he'd been a dockworker before becoming a vampire. His life had been hard, his upbringing rough, but no one would believe it now. Dressed for their run in shorts, a tank top, and running shoes, he seemed more a member of the country club crowd than the hard-nosed, hardworking crew he'd been a part of before his transition. It was easy for her to picture him on the golf course, hitting balls and zipping around in a golf cart. They did have glow-in-the-dark balls for such an occasion.

He was attractive enough in looks, but the chemistry between them had always been more friends than lovers.

She felt easier blaming their change of plans on Arthur than on her lack of strength. "Arthur has asked me to stay close to home. How about a video instead of a run? And we can take a swim later."

Luke shrugged. "Sure. Sounds like a wise move." He

scanned the nearby woods and mountainsides. "They may still be out there waiting for an opportunity. And I can't really imagine the Hamilton boys running with us."

Phoebe laughed at the image that popped into her head of the leather coiffed bikers running after them in their boots.

Purplish-gray clouds crept across the night sky and picked up the glow of the quarter moon curved above them. She itched to get her camera and try different ways of capturing the subtle light and colorful clouds. Maybe some other time.

She turned to find Luke studying her. Instead of the heavy something she expected, he said, "Okay. Rock-paper-scissors on the video."

She laughed. For some reason the idea of a vampire doing rock, paper, scissors seemed hilarious. "You'll have to teach me. I've never done rock-paper-scissors."

His eyes widened. "You're kidding."

She shook her head.

"You have been so sheltered," he complained.

That triggered her laughter again. She knew how to fight hand-to-hand, but had no idea how to do rock-paper-scissors.

Luke grinned and proceeded to describe what each hand position meant, and which topped the other. It took several tries before she won.

"Beginner's luck," he complained. "Unless you were

reading my mind."

She rolled her eyes. "Not one of my talents."

"What's it going to be?" he asked as they wandered into what they called the game room. The extra-large screen television, Blu-ray player, gaming system, and pool table took up just a small area of the room. Two long couches and two lounges were arranged in front of the television, and a bar where they could help themselves to refrigerated blood took up the other end.

"I could make you sit through a chick flick, but I know you hate them. So, since you let me win, I'm going to be kind."

He narrowed his green eyes. "What's it going to be?"

"*Terminator III.*"

"Yes!" Luke punctuated his shout with a fist pump.

"Good. You can deal with setting up the movie while I fix a drink. Do you want anything?"

"No. I'm good."

Though she had a cup of blood earlier, she selected a packet with her name on it from the refrigerator and fixed another. She'd need the added strength for the swim, as well as keeping up with things tomorrow. She stretched out on one of the two lounges.

Luke sat close by on the leather couch, kicked off his shoes, stretched his legs out, and propped his feet on the coffee table.

Phoebe did her best to pay attention to the movie, but

her meeting with Hunter Knox kept playing through her mind. How would he track Trevor? What steps would he take that she hadn't?

She had put out feelers to several clans across the state. So far no one had seen Trevor. He had to be laying low. But he still had to spend money to find a place to stay. The problem with most vampires was they paid for everything in cash.

It was hard to get a line of credit if you were dead.

And how did she go about annulling the marriage, since it had never been consummated, and her groom had *freaking tried to kill her*?

Surely attempted murder was grounds for annulment. She'd have to meet with Councilman Adcock to discuss it. The old crow. She wouldn't be above blackmailing him, if that was what it took to sever the connection to her husband.

The thought of Trevor possibly benefitting from her death threatened to blow the top of her head off.

But annulment of the contract might prove extremely complicated, since its purpose had been to bind their clans together in a sort of consortium. She needed to talk to Arthur about it and see what their options might be.

Luke interrupted her reverie. "Why did you choose to watch a video if you're going to stew all the way through it?"

"I'm not stewing, I'm thinking things through."

His light brown eyebrows shot up. "Care to share?"

"Not until I'm sure of the actions I want to take."

He reached for the remote and paused the movie. "It might help to talk it out."

She shook her head.

"You're going to be fine, Phoebe."

She wasn't going to give voice to the negative. "I'll fight until I can't. I don't know any other way."

His features went still, which he only did when he was deeply affected.

"We're going to figure this thing out. I promise you." He looked up at her, his expression regretful. "I wish I'd been here for the wedding. I might have been able to do something."

"Not unless you knew ahead of time that Trevor planned to murder me. I know Arthur needed you to go put out some fires with the outlying clans because of the contract."

"While you were facing off against Trevor, I was holding Malcolm Chester's hand, and reassuring him that the lines dividing the clans were not going to change, and that Ricci's clan wasn't going to take over. The comparison doesn't quite seem equal. If I'd have gotten even a whiff of trouble in the works, I wouldn't have gone."

She reached out to give his hand a squeeze. "It would have probably happened just the way it did even if you'd been here. And like you said, I'm going to get past this and get on with my life."

His fingers tightened over hers for a moment.

She turned her attention back to the big screen television. "Turn the movie back on."

"I'd rather go for that swim you mentioned. I need to blow off some steam."

"Okay. I'll go change."

Once she stood in her room, partially naked, and studied the large, dark area that wouldn't heal, fear stole the strength from her legs, and she slumped down on the end of the bed.

Being so close to death brought the memory of her original death boiling to the forefront, no matter how much she wished it had been erased from her memory during the process.

Her death would be forever this time.

She again forced her thoughts away from the negative, and went into the closet to get a scarf to cover her injury. If she could cover it so no one, including herself, could see it, maybe she could forget about it for a while.

She changed into the modest black one-piece she normally wore and grabbed a towel. Before she reached the door to the hall, her stomach roiled with nausea, and she rushed to the bathroom. The bright red blood tasted like death coming back up. Her stomach empty, she pressed a cool, damp cloth to the back of her neck because it was the human thing to do and she couldn't think of anything else to relieve the miserable aftermath of vomiting.

It did seem to help, and once the sickness passed, she brushed her teeth and tongue to remove the rancid taste in her mouth.

If one of the servants saw any evidence of her sickness, they would notify Arthur, so she gave the bathroom a quick cleaning. Then finally picked up her towel and headed back downstairs.

She heard Luke on the phone in the game room as she came down the stairs.

"No, she's about the same."

He was obviously talking about her.

"No. I don't want that at all. We'll talk about what needs to be done later."

Her curiosity was piqued, but she didn't want to tell him she'd been rude enough to listen to his private conversation.

"No, I'm trying to keep her mind off the problem right now. Trust me, you don't want her on your ass."

Who was he talking to?

"I don't need that kind of distraction." He paused to listen. "There's too much at stake, and we need to maintain focus on what's important."

What was he talking about? Since she'd been ill, Arthur had been cutting back on the things he asked her to do. It would be normal for him to ask Luke instead.

"If that was what you wanted, you should have waited. It's too late to regret it now."

She came to a standstill just outside the door. Uneasiness

crept up the back of her neck. Her normally slow-beating heart began to race.

He hung up the phone. She waited for a minute before walking into the room.

"Ready?" Luke asked, grabbing a towel off the back of the couch.

"Yes." The urge to ask straight out who he'd been talking to pushed against her teeth, but she bit it back. It had to be about a business deal. He wouldn't welcome her butting in.

The enclosed pool was bathed in steam, though neither of them had a body temperature to maintain. But the warmth did seem to do something for her skin. Maybe it would do something for her neck as well.

Luke's long body sliced the surface of the water like a knife. Phoebe chose to slide gently into the water from the steps at the shallow end. She slipped beneath the water, and was glad to find the chlorine seemed to have no adverse effect on her injury. In fact, the water seemed to sooth it a bit. Since she didn't need to breathe, she dropped down to the bottom of the pool and lay on her back to watch him swim up and down.

They had known each other so long, had both been adopted by Arthur as his children, and had worked with each other since the beginning. For all intents and purposes, Luke was her brother in every way. The idea that he would do anything to harm her or Arthur was unthinkable.

But right now she didn't know who she could trust, who might have been involved in the plot to take Arthur down. But it was feasible to think someone who knew them, who knew the house, could have helped Ricci.

They could have planted someone long before any of this went down. It didn't have to be someone who was involved in the infrastructure of the clan.

Arthur might still be in danger. Should something happen to him and wipe out those few at the top who held the clan together, chaos would reign. She was one of those at the top. Luke was one as well. Whoever it was, they had to have been promised something big. Power, money, a clan of his/her own.

The Stewart clan was more than just the vampires Arthur had created. It included homeless vampires who had settled here because he promised them protection and guidance.

She wanted to live, but there were others who would be affected by this situation. She'd never handled anything with the breadth and scope of what this poison could mean. She couldn't deal with it on her own.

Could Hunter Knox really help? Could he call upon more resources than she?

A figure appeared at the edge of the pool. Sophia, one of the young vampires in training, stood watching Luke while he did his laps, taking occasional sips from a glass. Phoebe had noticed her hanging about whenever she had a spare moment.

Luke swam to the side of the pool and rested his arms on the edge while they spoke. He accepted her glass, drank some, and returned it to her.

Luke was handsome, had a good sense of humor, and was very popular with the security trainees. He and Phoebe rarely talked about their romantic involvements, and if he was dating the young female, he'd never say anyway. But the two made a good pair.

Phoebe's thoughts returned to Hunter Knox. When he rested his hand against the small of her back, her legs had gone weaker than they already were. And there was that air of danger that set off all her sensual bells and whistles. Because danger was sexy.

She pressed her legs tightly together against the feeling of unrelieved need. It had been a long time since she'd been with a male.

But she mustn't get involved with Hunter. He was more than a private investigator. He was too polished, too focused. And then there was the Vampire Council poking into the fire at the wedding. If he were somehow a plant to dig into what had happened, she could be in some deep water. Deeper than she was already.

She had to stay strong until they found Trevor, and discovered who had betrayed them. It would be her swan song for the Stewart clan.

Then she could move on with her life as she had

planned.

She pushed off the bottom of the pool, and, reaching the surface, started her laps. As she swam, she blocked out Luke and Sophia's conversation, reluctant to intrude, though she caught the woman's strident tone when she said, "Why is she always with you?"

She finished her twentieth lap before Luke fell in beside her and matched his strokes with hers.

Chapter 6

ARTHUR STEWART GESTURED toward one of the leather couches in his study. "Please, have a seat, Agent Knox."

Hunter raised a brow at the address. Not detective but agent. Someone had talked out of turn. He sat down and waited while Arthur went to his desk to retrieve something. Stewart looked about Hunter's own human age, but was much older in vampire years. For all his grace and mild-mannered aplomb, there was an aura of power that resonated around him. You didn't screw with an eight-hundred-year-old vampire and get away with it. And someone had done just that.

When Stewart returned to sit down, he handed Hunter a folder.

"That is the guest list for the wedding. I've circled those who were burned in the fire. I've also included a copy of the contract Ricci and I signed before the wedding. Because of his betrayal, it will be voided during a National Council meeting next month, if the local Council can't do it.

Undoubtedly it would. Attempted murder of a master

vampire and his clan was definitely grounds for breach of contract and some legal proceedings. But should Phoebe die before then...

"As for the marriage, it is Phoebe's desire to have it annulled as soon as possible. In order to do that, she must go before the local Council, Adcock in particular. I will accompany her to the meeting and make certain she does nothing impulsive, because this will be the first time they meet since the wedding."

Hunter would love to be a bat on the wall for that meeting. "I agree it might be wise, sir."

Arthur nodded solemnly, but a small smile flashed across his face. "Phoebe will be down in a moment. The physician you sent, Dr. Graves, arrived half an hour ago to examine her."

"Despite his unfortunate name, Brady is one of the best human physicians I know. Since vampires are who we are, and most are arrogant enough to believe we are both indestructible and immortal, he specializes in anomalies within our species. There may be something he can do."

"I understand. We, too, have a human physician who sees to our needs on occasion."

"That's a very progressive stance, Mr. Stewart."

Arthur shrugged. "There has been a time or two in the past that I would have welcomed a helping hand, and there was never one there because of what I was. I want my people cared for." He folded his hands together. "To get back to Phoebe…She is very dear to me. She is my daughter in every way, including the blood that runs through her veins."

Shit. Hunter struggled to suppress the expletive. Arthur's message was loud and clear. No pressure there. "I understand."

"She will insist on accompanying you on your interviews. I will consider it a personal favor to me if you will allow her to do so. She needs to be an active participant in fighting for her life. If she's forced to remain here in a passive role, she will either go mad or do something rash."

She didn't seem rash at all. She seemed driven. But he didn't know her that well…yet. "I'm not certain my boss will agree to that."

"I have already discussed this with Vladimir, and you will be receiving a text with special permission."

"So I surmised when you greeted me as Agent Knox."

"I know every vampire in my district. You aren't one of them. So I called Vladimir."

Shit. He needed to talk to his boss ASAP. Vlad at least owed him an explanation for breaking his cover. Damn him.

"I would rather Phoebe not know what agency I work for, Mr. Stewart. She will probably be more open to answering my questions if you keep it between us. Suspects and victims alike hear the words National Vampire Security Council and automatically go into cover-their-ass mode."

"Phoebe has no reason to do that. She's the victim here.

Even if I avoid telling her, she'll discover it herself, if she hasn't already. She's very resourceful and shrewd."

"I'm sure I wouldn't be surprised at all, sir. She seems very...capable. But the other thing is, I work best alone."

"Perhaps it's time you learned to share the workload."

"It's a conflict of interest for her to investigate her own case, and if it goes before the National Council, they will be able to throw it out because she had access to the evidence. It will muddy the waters."

"All she wants to do is find Trevor Ricci and get the poison antidote. Who would work harder than she will? She has a stronger incentive to find him than anyone else, because her life depends on it."

"I'm aware of that. But, and I don't mean any disrespect to her or to make light of her situation when I say this, her life is not the only one at risk here. If Trevor Ricci has discovered a poison that can kill us, there is nothing to stop him from selling it to others who wish to do the same to their enemies or their competitors. And should the humans gain control of it..."

"We have thought about all that, Mr. Knox." Phoebe spoke from the doorway.

He'd been so intent on his effort to talk Stewart out of her joining him, he hadn't heard her and Luke arrive.

Phoebe thrust her fingers through the thick strands of multicolored hair around her face and brushed them back. She looked paler with the darkening circles beneath her eyes and the growing bruise on her neck. "I have something no one else has that might help us hunt Trevor down."

"What's that?"

"I drank his blood at the wedding two days ago. I may be able to track him."

✧　✧　✧

PHOEBE WATCHED WHILE Hunter gripped the steering wheel with exquisite control, changed gears, and increased the speed. The Jaguar raced down the curving mountain road with the grace of the powerful jungle cat for which it was named. The heavily leafed trees on either side flashed by, while moonlight threw splotches of shadow over the windshield.

"The chances you'll be able to track Trevor are slim," he warned.

She could practically feel the anger wafting off of him.

"Why are you opposed to trying?"

He glanced at her. "I'm not. I just didn't want you to get your hopes up."

They both knew it wasn't what had triggered this taut, controlled resentment.

"I have an appointment at Have Wand, Will Travel with Calamity's boss, Zaira. If you can drop me there, I'd appreciate it."

"I thought they were off the case."

"They are. This is something else I'm following up on."

He shot her another quick glance, but turned toward town as soon as they pulled onto the main road. Once he reached the agency's parking lot, he whipped into it, put the car in park, and turned off the engine.

"Thanks for the lift. I'll go my own way from here. Arthur need never know we parted company. I know he's given you enough information to start with, and I hope it will lead you to something helpful." She released her seat belt and reached for the door handle.

Hunter grasped her arm. "You really expect us to go our separate ways?"

She studied his masculine face. "Yes, I do."

"Why?" He eyed her with interest.

"Because you'll stand in my way."

His brows rose and he pointed at himself with a long, blunt-tipped finger. "*I'll* stand in *your* way."

"Yeah. Men can't help themselves. Everything is about ego to them. And right now you're pissed because you've been told to drag me around with you. My time may be short, and my temper's even shorter when it comes to bullshit. So I'm relieving you of your burden. You go your way, and I'll go mine. The first vampire to find Trevor can inform the other."

"And you're here to see Zaira because?" he asked.

"She's a witch. A very powerful healing witch. I don't expect her to be able to heal me, but she may buy me a few extra days." There were other things she hoped to try that had occurred to her during the long hours she'd spent obsessing over her situation. She'd discussed them all with Zaira.

She opened the car door. By the time she stepped out of the vehicle, Hunter was beside her.

She studied him for a long moment. His gray gaze remained steady on her face. Her stomach did a slow tumble, and an insistent tingle ignited between her legs. How could she respond to him physically with this poison ravaging her system? She knew it was. She'd been so weak this evening, only Arthur's fresh blood had made it possible for her to rise.

"I think I'd like to stick around to make sure you're okay, during and after the spell she's going to try."

Damn. She'd hoped he'd get his fine ass back in the car and drive away. She strode toward the front of the building. "I've let you off the hook. You don't have to stay."

"Your sire put you in my hands for safekeeping."

She humphed, turned, and stalked across the parking lot.

Hunter caught up to her in a nanosecond. "You don't think I can keep you safe?"

"I don't think I need you to."

"You couldn't defend yourself against Trevor, could you?"

She stopped. A quick rush of anger left her cheeks prickling with heat. She had defended herself and Arthur, but she couldn't tell him about it. "Not after the initial poisoning. No. But there's nothing to keep me from ripping his throat out now."

"We need the poison and information about it beforehand, Phoebe. We men may be all about ego, but women are driven by emotion. Do you really trust yourself to meet him face-to-face and not rip his face off?"

"I think I can keep it together until I have what I need. After that, I don't want you around to interfere with me while I do what I need to do."

"After we have what we need, I'll lock the door and stand guard until you've exacted your revenge."

She studied him long and hard through narrowed eyes. Damn him. She was well aware of her weaknesses now. And the truth was, she needed his help in case she found herself too debilitated to go on alone. "Swear on your sire's life."

He placed his hand over his heart. "I swear on my sire, Vladimer Tepes', life, I will allow you to exact your revenge on the man responsible for poisoning you."

"Vlad Tepes is dead. He can't be your sire."

"It's interesting that you know your history, but that was his grandson."

"I want to meet him."

"You don't believe me?" he asked, his smile one of open amusement.

"No. I don't."

He shook his head. "You don't even know me, and have already decided I'm a liar." He reached for the door and opened it for her.

He might be a liar, but she couldn't fault his manners. "You don't know me either, but you'd already decided I was going to be a burden before we left the house." She shrugged. Her shoulders were aching after just that small movement. In fact, her whole body was aching.

Christophe Bakas, Zaira's vampire boyfriend, was hanging out in the reception area. His dark curly hair tumbled across his forehead in handsome disarray, and he smiled at Phoebe while approaching her with an extended hand. "It's good to see you, Phoebe. Zaira is preparing for the spell. I thought I'd hang around in case either of you needed my help."

"Thank you, Christophe. I appreciate it."

Zaira's dog Cerbie padded his way down the hall. The Jack Russell was shaped like an overstuffed tube sock with a nose on one end and a stubby tail on the other. Cerbie wiggled his way up to Phoebe and rubbed against her legs in a bid for attention.

She leaned down to rub him behind the ears and spoke to him. He did his funny growl, grunt thing which meant he was in a state of utter doggie bliss, his tail vibrating like a tuning fork.

When Phoebe moved into her house, she planned to get a dog. A pet would provide company and unconditional love, and would never pass her off to someone else. "You got any buddies who need a home, Cerbie?" she asked. The little fellow sat down in front of her and cocked his head, as though giving the question some thought.

She straightened when Zaira appeared in the doorway. "I'm ready for you, Phoebe."

She turned to Hunter. "You can stay here with Calamity and Cerbie until we're done."

"I don't think so, Phoebe." He bent to allow Cerbie to sniff his hand, but his attention rested on her.

She crossed her arms and raised a brow.

"I'm not leaving you, Phoebe." He gave Cerbie a scratch behind the ears.

Damnit. He was so intense, with his gray eyes and kissable mouth, and she was so drawn to him. She couldn't act on it when she might only have a few days or weeks to live. She didn't need the distraction when she was looking for Trevor. *Her husband. The asshat rat bastard.*

"I don't want to hear a single negative thing while we're working."

He bent his head in a very old-fashioned manner. "Word of honor."

She swiveled on one booted heel back to Zaira. "Let's do this."

There were those who believed the undead no longer experienced human emotions or responded to emotional upheaval as the living did. But after she sat down, Phoebe kept her hands clamped on the arms of the desk chair to still their shaking.

She needed this healing more than she needed blood,

more than she'd ever needed anything in her life. Even more than sunshine.

Zaira's auburn hair hung down her back in a long braid, its rich, dark color contrasting with her pale, flawless skin. She studied the bite on Phoebe's neck for several minutes, a crease between her brows.

Phoebe rushed to say, "It's poison, Zaira. If there might be any danger to you at all, I'd rather you not try."

"There won't be. I promise. I'm going to attempt to draw the poison free of your system and into a beaker. It will take several minutes and it will probably be very uncomfortable."

"Whatever you can do…. I'm willing to take the risk."

Zaira nodded. "I worked on this spell last night, and I've made it as safe as I can for both of us. I called several friends to ask their opinion, and they seemed to think it would be okay."

The concern on the other woman's face triggered an unfamiliar rush of fear. Phoebe's heart began to pound. "You know your magic so I'm sure it will be fine."

Zaira turned away to get a ceremonial knife. "Before we do this spell, I'd like to attempt a locator spell. If that's unsuccessful, I can guide you while you attempt to find him yourself."

"Okay."

"All I need is a little blood."

"I'll handle that for you, Zaira," Chris said.

"No." Phoebe stood. "We don't know what concentration of poison is in my blood, and what quantity is harmful. All I did was taste the residue on Trevor's skin and it nearly killed me, Chris. I won't ask anyone else to take such a risk."

His concern was easy to read. "Thank you. I appreciate it."

Zaira touched his arm. "Spread the map out on my desk, Chris. Phoebe can prick her own wrist."

Chris and Hunter spread out the map and weighted the corners with small objects from a shelf behind it.

Zaira handed her a small ceremonial knife. "I need you to cut your wrist just a little and let a few drops of blood drip out onto the map."

Phoebe quickly nicked a vein and allowed a small amount of blood to drop onto the laminated surface. She set aside the knife and grabbed a tissue to put pressure on the wound. It would heal quickly. Or at least it would have in the past. She didn't know if the poison would keep it from happening this time.

Zaira stood over the map and held her hand over it.

"From their first night,

The groom took flight.

A husband he was to be,

But now his spouse he does not see.

The bond is broken,

The vows a token.

To insure she may be free,

Let us see,

Wherever he might be.

So mote it be."

The small pool of blood moved sluggishly in a swirl, then merged together into a cohesive ball the size of a marble. It perched there, as though held in place by a magnet.

Zaira looked up, her expression apologetic. "He's either here in Scryville, or the amount of his blood in your system isn't enough to track him this way."

Phoebe bit back a frustrated expletive. "I suspected as much. But thank you for trying." She wiped up the blood with the tissue now the puncture on her wrist had closed, and tossed the stained paper into the trashcan next to the desk.

She and Zaira exchanged a glance. She'd burn it before leaving the office.

Phoebe squared her shoulders. "I want to try tracking him the way we discussed."

Zaira patted the back of the desk chair. "Have a seat."

Phoebe wiggled back into the leather seat and closed her eyes, then shook her arms and rolled her neck to relax.

"Just rest a moment. Try to wipe your mind free of everything weighing on it. You're in a safe place. A place comfortable and warm." Zaira's voice droned on slow and hypnotic as she eased Phoebe into a light trance.

Phoebe flashed back to the image of Hunter beneath the streetlights, standing so close before they entered the office. She'd been touched by the concern in his expression and the protectiveness of his posture.

She pushed the strong impression away and wrestled her mind back to focusing on Trevor.

Zaira's voice guided her. "Imagine Trevor is standing in front of you."

Phoebe visualized his eyes, the line of his jaw, the way his hair fell forward and to the side. Blackness swirled behind her eyelids until his image appeared like a ghost, transparent and insubstantial. He sat at a table or desk talking to someone. He suddenly stopped and looked around the room, as though he sensed her watching him. Goose bumps rushed over her skin, and the hair on the back of her neck rose. Could he sense her? See her as she was seeing him?

She concentrated on his location. Cream walls, a round table, and the impression of a small space led her to think it might be an inexpensive room. Light-blocking curtains hung closed next to the table. "He's northeast, not so far away." She had no idea how she knew.

"Are you sure?" Hunter spoke for the first time since they entered the room.

"A hotel, possibly. Is there a hotel nearby patronized by vampires?"

"A few."

"Not an expensive place. He's with someone, and they're talking. I can see the other vampire's hands. They aren't Ricci's. He has fingers like fat sausages."

"Concentrate on Trevor, Phoebe," Zaira urged. "Or you may lose the connection."

"He doesn't look like his normal well-groomed self. His shirt's wrinkled, and his hair is mussed."

Trevor beckoned to someone nearby, and a woman plodded to the table hesitantly. He commanded her to kneel. Her face, young and tender, came into focus. She wasn't a woman, but a girl of fifteen or sixteen, with an unfocused, distant expression. Oh, no. She'd been compelled. He tilted her head to the side, leaned down, and struck.

Phoebe's stomach muscles contracted, and her fingers tightened over the arms of the desk chair. The girl was too young, and had not gone to Trevor willingly.

The attack that left Phoebe clinging to life replayed through her head, and she gritted her teeth against the overwhelming urge to yell at him to stop.

Trevor straightened, wiped his mouth with his sleeve, and shoved the girl away. She fell to the floor, out of sight.

He accepted a deck of cards from the other man and began shuffling them. They were playing cards. Playing cards while the girl lay dying because he had fed too deeply. Rage flared along her nerve endings like electricity, and she gripped the arms of the chair harder. The plastic cracked.

"Phoebe," Hunter's voice broke into her concentration

with a note of warning.

She concentrated on the playing cards. She wanted to set fire to them and Trevor. Wanted it with everything in her being. Heat inside her body started to rise, but she beat it back. She would wait until she had the poison. Then he was toast.

She opened her eyes. "We need to go."

Zaira laid a hand on her arm. "We need to drain as much poison from your blood as possible first, Phoebe."

"There's a young girl in that room. Trevor fed from her, and now she's unconscious. She could be dying."

Hunter swore.

"Could we use the poison as a conduit to find Trevor?"

Zaira frowned. "If he has it on him, possibly. But there's no guarantee."

"Damnit!" And there was no guarantee they could find him in time to save the girl, even if Phoebe could tell them where he was.

She'd never attempted to start a fire long distance, but then she'd never had a connection to direct it through. Phoebe closed her eyes and drew a deep, cleansing breath as Zaira had instructed her earlier. She focused on Trevor again. His image came through more clearly this time. She embraced the human, psychic part of her. Heat rampaged through her, building as she drew it in from the elements around her. She let it build until a spark ignited, and she shoved it down the connection, directly at him.

The cards in Trevor's hand burst into flame. He screamed like a girl and hurled them away. Leaping across the table, he landed in a crouch, his eyes darting around the room. Then he rushed to the door, jerked it open, and poked his head out. An oval sign glowed yellow and orange, a huge moon against a dark purple background.

She recognized the sign, having passed it every time she went out of town.

"They're at the Full Moon. I don't know what room. We need to hurry."

Hunter pushed against her shoulder, holding her in place easily, though she struggled against it. "Chris and I will take care of this. You need to stay and let Zaira do what she can for you."

He and Chris sped out of the room, the door waving back and forth in their wake.

"Damn it. They won't make it in time."

"What did you do, Phoebe?" Zaira asked. "I was across the room when I felt the push of power."

She'd known Zaira almost as long as she had Calamity, but only Zaira and Zelda knew about her special gifts, gifts she brought with her through her transition. She studied Zaira's face for several seconds. "They say gambling is a sin and will send you to hell. I just gave them a little taste of what they may be in for."

Zaira laughed, then just as quickly grew sober. "You may have given up your chance to catch Trevor so you could save the girl."

Phoebe nodded. "She's just a kid. Too young to die, and too young to turn. I hope Trevor and his cohort bugged out and left her behind."

"Chris will call and let me know. He's good about things like that."

"I don't think Hunter will. He strikes me as the type you'd have to torture to get answers from, and then you might not get them anyway."

"Roger says pretty much the same thing. If you have a secret, though, he'll ferret it out. He's that good."

Was Zaira warning her, or just repeating what Roger said?

"Then I suppose I'd better make certain I've paid him a retainer, so he's under contract, and can't reveal anything that happens while we're together."

"A retainer might be a good idea."

It was already too late. He'd witnessed what happened here, and he'd realize what she'd done once he and Chris arrived at the hotel.

Chapter 7

HUNTER DROVE THE Jaguar full out while it growled its way through back roads, all the way across town to the Full Moon Hotel. The squat, two-story building with exterior walkways had the look of cheesy seventies architecture, except heavy steel doors and bulletproof windows replaced the flimsy originals, and extra-thick privacy curtains covered the windows—both to make sure the glow of lights inside the rooms didn't show at night, and the sun didn't intrude during the day.

Hunter whipped into the parking lot. The car slid to a stop, kicking up gravel at the front door just as he and Chris leapt out of the car and rushed into the office.

The young shifter working the desk shook his head, his eyes wide at their questions. "I can't tell you what room any guest is in. It's against policy."

Every second this kid kept them away from Trevor's room, the girl could be getting closer to death. And Trevor and his companion would be getting farther and farther away.

Hunter's frustration bubbled over. He grabbed the kid,

dragged him across the desk, shoved him against the waist-high counter, and stuck the picture of Trevor in his face. "This asshole has kidnapped a young human girl, and is feeding on her as we speak. If you don't give me his room number, I'm going to pull the fire alarm and get the human fire department out here. You don't want anyone to get interested in the things going on behind some of these doors, but if the humans show up, they will be paying attention, believe me. Give us the number, and we can avoid that."

The young shifter's eyes were big as the moon on the sign outside. "It's room two-nineteen."

"Chris, kill the phone," Hunter ordered. "If they're still in the room, we don't want Mr. Policy here calling to warn them."

Hunter didn't wait for him, but charged out of the office, scanning the parking lot and the cars. The place was full. He rushed up the concrete stairs with its flimsy white wrought iron railing, and only had to wait a moment before Chris was beside him, waving an extra key to the door. The vamp was proving to be a competent partner.

Hunter kept his voice to less than a whisper, knowing the other man could hear him. "Be careful. They may have the poison, and I don't have to tell you they're dangerous."

Chris answered in kind, "I may be a nerdy college professor, but I can handle myself."

"Good. Open the door from the side. I'll go in first."

Chris stuck the electronic key into the lock and twisted the door handle. Hunter went in fast, crouching as he scanned the room. It was empty, but for the young girl sprawled on the floor. Bruises covered her arms, and raw puncture on her throat wounds still seeped blood. He quickly moved to her side and checked for a pulse. "She's still alive, but her pulse is weak. We need to contact emergency services."

"I'll call it in to ours," Chris jerked a cell phone out of his pocket.

Hunter prowled the room for evidence of Trevor's occupancy. The room was neat, the beds made, the only evidence anyone had been there a pile of towels on the bathroom floor, a still-dripping shower stall, and a dying girl.

"EMSV is coming." Chris murmured. "They'll give her a transfusion and drop her off in front of her house."

"Good." Hunter bent and found three partially burned scraps of paper under the table. He studied the images printed on them. Phoebe had said Trevor and another man were playing cards. Why would they burn their cards?

Hunter stuffed them in his pocket. "Are you okay to stay with her while I go back and talk to the desk clerk?"

"Sure."

The young desk clerk dodged behind the desk when he saw Hunter coming. "Stay away from me."

"We've called EMSV to come and treat the victim. She's alive, but just barely. The vampires who were in the room, did you see where they went?"

The kid looked like he might refuse to answer, then his shoulders fell. "They arrived in a dark green jeep two days ago. It shot out of the parking lot just before you got here, heading west."

"Did you get the license plate number?"

"No. We don't do that. It might infringe on our guests' privacy."

Hunter was well versed in how secretive vampires, shifters, and other groups could be. It made it hard as hell to track them. And they'd just missed catching the vamp responsible for Phoebe's poisoning.

An ambulance sped into the parking lot.

"You do realize you saved the girl's life by cooperating with us. Her death could have created major issues for us all. They'll treat her, compel her to forget, and she'll go on with her life none the wiser. Which will be a kindness to her."

The clerk nodded, a thick hank of hair bobbing against his forehead.

Hunter left the kid and walked out to find the EMTs already loading the girl into the ambulance. A small crowd had gathered. He smelled shifters, and a hint of faerie. And was that foul scent gnome? He hadn't run across one of them in years. He realized he was reaching for something—anything—to think about but the woman they left in Zaira's office, and what this would mean for her.

Chris wandered up. "The girl's going to be okay."

"Good. I hope Phoebe will be, too. She gave up an opportunity for us to catch these bastards in order to save the girl's life."

✧ ✧ ✧

ZAIRA PLACED A metal bowl on the desk standing in the middle of the circle she closed around them. Several bowls filled with ground herbs and flowers also sat on the desk. Phoebe caught the scent of sage among several others she couldn't identify. Candles flickered at the four corners.

Zaira dipped a ceremonial dagger into the water she'd just purified, then used it to scrape the ground herbs and flowers into another bowl. Mixing some of the purified water into the blend, she made a paste. With the tip of the blade, she applied it to the puncture wounds on Phoebe's neck.

She moved the tip of the blade in a counterclockwise circle around and around the bite without touching the skin.

"Within her body lies

A poison that tries

To end her life,

So draw this knife,

And with her stillness

I'll pull free this illness,

And let us face

This evil trace,

By the Goddess I decree,

So mote it be."

A drawing sensation surrounded the bite mark like a string that had worked its way to the surface of her skin and was being pulled out of the wound. The spasm of pain which struck her was so intense Phoebe's grip on the chair arm tightened again, and the plastic finally shattered and crumbled. She clutched the metal frame that was left, trying to twist away from the excruciating pain, but, other than her hands, she couldn't move her body. Completely in the grasp of Zaira's magic, she closed her eyes and gritted her teeth.

Zaira shoved a bowl against her neck beneath the wound.

The hot feeling of fluid flowing out of the bite made Phoebe itch. Everything in her body was draining out the small puncture wounds in her neck. Every inch of her screamed with pain. It took all the control she had to avoid shrieking in agony, and tears streamed down her face while a strangled sound ripped out of her.

Zaira said, "It's almost over, Phoebe."

She prayed to the Goddess it was, because she didn't think she could bear it much longer without shattering.

Zaira set aside the bowl and reached for a towel to blot her neck.

"This spell must end.

Please heal this friend,

And set her free.

So mote it be."

While Zaira's last words were still resonating in the room, Phoebe lunged up and out of the chair, sending Zaira stumbling back out of her way. Dizziness drove Phoebe to one knee. She braced her hands on the floor while tears continued to run down her face to drip off her chin. In moments her head cleared, and she pushed shakily to her feet.

She opened her eyes to see Zaira's worried gaze fastened on her. "How do you feel?" The witch handed her some tissues.

While she wiped her face, Phoebe took stock. Her body no longer ached, and the constant throb of the bite had receded to a weak twinge. "Better. I think." She gritted her teeth. "You said uncomfortable."

"I'm sorry. I thought if I told you the truth, it would only have made it worse leading up to it."

"Worse!" She shook her head.

Zaira moved on. "We have another problem."

Having barely recovered from the torture, she didn't want to hear about another problem. But didn't have the luxury of ignoring whatever it was. "What is it?"

"There's more poison in the bowl than you could have

ingested from one small bite from Trevor's neck. And I can't guarantee I got it all."

Phoebe crossed the short distance and looked in the metal vessel. About the size of her childhood favorite cereal bowl, the container was nearly full of a thick, cloudy fluid. She'd been drinking more blood lately than anyone else at the house, but only drank her own supply, which had her name written on it. Why had she not died?

"Dear Goddess." She whipped her cell phone out, swiped the screen to unlock it, and hit the number she needed most. "Arthur, our blood bank may have been compromised. Tell everyone at the house not to drink any more until it's tested.

"And make sure everything with my name on it is destroyed. I think someone there has added small doses of the poison to it. Zaira just drained a bowlful from me." She took a deep breath. "The only thing that's been keeping me alive is your blood, Arthur. It's been counteracting the poison, or at least beating it back."

Chapter 8

DESPITE HUNTER'S EFFORTS to start a conversation with Phoebe a time or two, the silence between them stretched for the last twenty miles of the drive back to Scryville. The docs hadn't been overly encouraging, but they did extend a ray of hope. Until they found a pure sample of the substance to use for developing an antidote, it was better than nothing.

And there was another finding that relieved him. The poison couldn't be absorbed through the skin and only activated when it mixed with blood. Thus the reason why Trevor had rubbed the wound on Phoebe's neck after he bit her. He'd introduced poison into her system. Having her bite him and suck the poison from his skin with it had given her a double dose. She'd have died on the stage without the antidote and Arthur Stewart's blood.

He had seldom been more confused by a case and the vampires involved.

Stewart felt deep affection for Phoebe. He had read that in the Master Vampire's demeanor and his concern. But why had he so carelessly handed her off to Trevor Ricci?

Trevor was brilliant at business, but his reputation for cruelty and spiteful behavior held him back. Phoebe also had business acumen, as well as a gift for creating bridges between vampire and other species' interests. She would have been the perfect choice if Stewart planned a hostile takeover of Ricci's clan.

If that was the case, Phoebe had to know about the plan. But she didn't strike him as devious.

Or was that wishful thinking on his part? He wanted her to be the upright female she seemed to be. He shrugged to himself. If she knew what her sire had planned, he'd find out about it soon enough.

It was a relief when Phoebe's cell phone rang.

He listened to both sides of their conversation, and pieced together what she was talking about and who she was talking to when she called the man Luke.

Hunter already begun building more detailed, in-depth dossiers than what Arthur gave him on all the vampires and servants who worked and lived in his house.

Luke Jakes was third in command after Phoebe in Stewart's business empire. And it was an empire.

Aside from those three, there were very few vampires who worked at the house. Five humans worked there—the housekeeper; Arthur's personal servant Horacio, who had been with him at least two hundred years; Luke Jakes' personal servant, Thaddeus; and two women who came in to clean.

Phoebe had no staff of her own.

She had an independent streak a mile wide, and quite a temper. He could see the rage working through her even now.

She disconnected the call and turned to him. "They've tested all the blood at the house and decided to stick with live donors until we can find out who's contaminating it. Luckily no one else's supply was touched. As far as we can tell."

So she remained the sole target so far, which he found troubling. "Sounds like a wise thing to do."

"Thank you taking the poison Zaira drained out of me to the lab."

"It's part of my job. I've put out a bolo on the green jeep and Trevor to my contacts all over the state in regular human law enforcement and the preternatural community."

"I'm relieved to hear it. Zaira's bought me some time, but the scientists say an undiluted sample of the poison would go a long way toward creating a true antidote. As of now they suspect the poison might have been changed by ingestion, just enough to make their analysis less exact."

"Your color is much better, and the bite has partially healed. Zaira's a powerful witch. Powerful enough to do more than work as a PI."

"She's been approached by the Council of Magic Beings to do other things, but she doesn't want to get tied up in the politics."

"I understand." He glanced in her direction and paused to study her profile. He needed to break down the barriers between them to get at the heart of this case. "I'll concede that I behaved like an ass earlier tonight when we first left the house."

"Yes, you did." Amusement twitched at corners of her mouth and eyes.

He smiled. "You don't give an inch, do you?"

"No, but you just did."

Darlin' I could give you a lot more than that. Hunter bit the inside of his lip to keep from smiling, but he couldn't control his physical response to her.

"One of my gifts is reading minds."

Hunter laughed. "We both know that isn't true."

"How do you know?"

He shot her a heated glance. "If it was, you'd be wiggling in your seat right now with your panties on fire."

For the first time he saw her poise falter. She bowed her head, and her hair fell forward to hide her expression. She suddenly laughed, the sound husky, uninhibited, and sexy as hell. He got harder.

When she glanced up, one wing of blond hair lay against her cheek, and a smile still lingered.

He was disappointed when she turned to look out the side window without comment.

PHOEBE HAD NEVER reacted to a male the way she did to Hunter. But she had to be cautious. In fairness, she shouldn't start something she might not have time to finish.

Being vampire was supposed to mean being impervious to disease and able to heal quickly, but it left options for more human entertainments less compelling. She could party, but drugs and alcohol had no effect on her. She really liked having a drink now and then. Just one. She'd been so conservative as a human. Now she wished she'd cut loose and gotten drunk at least once. She would have enjoyed the easy feeling of euphoria humans described to her.

Fighting, killing, hunting, and sex seemed to be the norm among her current species. Violence seemed to fulfill their need to feel alive in some way. She understood the drive. Because of her gift, she still retained a tiny bit of human, and it somehow helped her avoid succumbing completely to vampire norms.

Pouring her time and concentration into her responsibilities to Arthur's corporation helped. Her photography gave her a more creative outlet.

Her few romantic relationships over the years hadn't worked for long. With immortality came restlessness, and the males were seldom satisfied. There was so much more out there, and an eternity in which to enjoy it. What might have lasted a lifetime, had they been human, always ended up being a short-term affair, and left her feeling rejected and hurt, but also less than what she was. Romance wasn't worth it.

But her attraction to this male sitting beside her was hard to ignore. He smelled of some light cologne and him, an earthy, masculine scent she wanted to breathe in and savor. He had a focus and strength she was drawn to. Like Arthur's.

But she couldn't encourage him or let herself fall into something when she might have so little time left. If she survived, maybe then she could pursue this. Once she wasn't married anymore.

And that led her right back to her situation with Trevor. Rage, bone deep and hot as hellfire, scorched through her. Bottom line, his attempt to kill her was nothing more than a quick and easy way to discard her, just as every other male in her life had done.

But he'd put a whole new spin on ending their relationship. Most guys just told her it wasn't working for them and walked away.

He'd freaking tried to kill her. The dickweed.

But that didn't mean she couldn't simply have sex with Hunter. He was attracted to her and attractive. Hell, he was more than attractive, he was...breathtakingly male, sexy, and there was an aura of danger about him. All that controlled power and strength could add a whole dimension to bed sport. She needed to feel alive. She needed to be held.

She needed to not be alone.

She wasn't safe in her own home. What was to keep

whoever had added poison to her blood supply from slipping into her room and staking her while she slept?

Although some of the others were able to resist the pull of sunrise for a short time, she died very quickly at dawn. Arthur could even walk outside in daylight without burning. Luke had a few minutes past dawn, but still couldn't go out into direct sunlight. She didn't know about the others. But the humans were awake all the time. The doors at the house, for all their added strength and security, wouldn't deter someone determined to breach one, and it would be easy to...

"Hunter... I don't want to go back to the house." She couldn't believe she was saying it.

He glanced in her direction. "Where would you like to go?"

She swallowed the knot of emotion stuck in her throat. Where could she go? Her house wasn't ready yet. "Arthur has a cabin out by the lake. I want to stay there tonight."

"Alone?"

"Yes. No one will know I'm there."

He frowned. "Do you want to go home and pick up some things?"

"No. I'd like to stop by Grayson's. They're open twenty-four/seven, so I can run in and pick up what I need, and it's right on the way."

"And what about food, Phoebe?"

"I'll be okay for a few days."

"You heard what the lab guy said. Feeding dilutes the poison and helps your system keep it suppressed. You can't go without feeding."

"I can't go back to the house. I'm vulnerable there after sundown." She glanced at her watch. "And we'll only just make it to the cabin in time for you to drop me off and make it back to Scryville."

"Unless I stay," he suggested.

Her heartbeat rose and her body warmed to the suggestion, though she ignored it. "I'm not doing this to instigate some kind of hookup. I don't feel safe at the house anymore." Damn, she'd acknowledged her attraction to him with that statement. Would he pick up on the slip?

"I wouldn't be staying to instigate some kind of hookup. I'd be there for your protection."

She studied his profile for a long moment. When he finally looked at her, every hint of flirtation had been swallowed up by his intense focus. He was all business.

"You don't have to stay. No one will know I'm there. Well, no one but Arthur. I'll need to call him. I promised to check in."

Hunter flipped out his phone. "What's the address? I'll need to know the GPS coordinates so I can meet the person bringing supplies somewhere along the way."

"Supplies?" Why was she getting the feeling things were getting out of hand?

"Food and some clothing."

"Who will we be meeting?"

"My personal assistant."

"Assistant?"

"Yes. Ancil takes care of my office, accounting, and a few other things while I'm out in the field. He's a jack of all trades."

He was a stranger. He'd have no reason to be part of any of this. "How long has he been with you?"

"Eighty years."

Phoebe gave him the address.

He dialed the number and hit the speaker. A man's voice filled the car. "What may I do for you, Hunter?"

"I need you to meet me out on Shady Valley Road at..." Hunter waited for Phoebe to speak.

"There's a store called Johnson's Pit Stop. They're shifters, but very welcoming."

"Thank you, ma'am. What do you need me to bring?"

"Four packages of O negative and my emergency kit. You'll probably reach the store before we do. We'll be there as quickly as possible."

"I will see you there." Ancil hung up.

"Emergency kit?" Phoebe asked.

"I'm sometimes called out unexpectedly, and keep a bag packed for just such an occasion. Now I need directions to Grayson's."

"Make a right up ahead, and we can take back roads to the store."

Fifteen minutes later Hunter pulled up before a sprawling cinderblock structure.

"You can buy anything in Grayson's. They have things inside here I never dreamed they would."

"Like Wal-Mart?"

She shook her head. "Not even close! It's like Wal-Mart on crack."

"Sounds like you enjoy coming here." Hunter had a look of dread on his face.

Typical male. His assistant probably bought his clothes. Men hated to shop.

Phoebe grinned. "I love shopping here. But I'll only go in and buy exactly what I need for tonight and tomorrow."

He didn't look convinced.

He was so serious. Did he ever relax? "Come in with me."

"I think I'd better." He climbed out of the car to join Phoebe. "I don't want to be caught in the car when the sun comes up."

Phoebe laughed and impulsively grabbed his hand. "You're going to like it. I promise."

"SHIT!" HUNTER STOPPED at the door, shocked at the depth of the building and how much of everything there was. Huge signs designated each department, just like any other large-scale department store, but there was also furniture at one end, and a rental area for everything from carpet shampooers to tools to smaller things. And the food court positioned to the left of the main entrance had a booming business going, even at three in the morning.

Phoebe got a small basket. "I usually get my shopping done in under fifteen minutes. But then I end up wandering around people-watching and taking it all in." She led the way to women's clothing and quickly selected serviceable-looking underwear, socks, a nightshirt, a pair of jeans, a sweater and a T-shirt, apparently unconcerned about the style or name brand of the items. In the pharmacy area, she snagged a toothbrush and toothpaste, then zipped over to beauty aids for a hairbrush and chap stick. She paid for everything at the pharmacy.

"There's even a weapons section?" Hunter mused while they wandered the perimeter of the store. "Guns, bows, knives, Tasers, pepper spray, bulletproof vests. Anything you'd need to protect yourself."

"Do you do your own shopping?" she asked.

"Not often. Ancil keeps me supplied with what I need, and the company I work for supplies me with transportation and weapons when I need them."

"Weapons?"

"Some of the cases I've dealt with involve other species. They sometimes require more than brute strength to control."

"I have spent more time in my work building bridges

between species."

He had done some research on his own after meeting with Phoebe last night. By the time he finished, he saw how bad a choice she had been to use as a pawn in the kind of situation Arthur Stewart was trying to manipulate. If his goal had been to win over the Ricci clan instead...she'd have been perfect.

Arthur Stewart had endangered someone valuable to their whole species with his choices.

"There's an art gallery with local artwork displayed over next to the food court." She pointed to the west front corner. "A tattoo parlor in the east back corner, and a pet department, with a dog groomer and a veterinarian, in the back west.

"And then there's Dreamland straight ahead," she added with a twinkle.

"Dreamland."

"Yes." She smiled as they came to a stop before double glass doors with an "Eighteen and Over" sign painted in bold letters across them.

"Would that happen to be where you got the leather bustier and pants you wore at the wedding?"

"Yes, it is."

Had she bought them for Trevor or had she worn them before? A strange feeling overwhelmed him, and he found himself grinding his teeth.

"I bought a formal dress for the wedding, but after Arthur came to my room to discuss what Trevor's expectations might be afterward, I zoomed over here on my motorcycle and got them. You watched the video?"

So she hadn't worn them for anyone else. He drew a deep breath and relaxed his jaw. "Yes, I watched the recording."

"I wanted to scare the shit out of him, so he'd want to get as far away from me as possible the minute the 'I do's' were said. I was thinking the other end of the state, not from here to the hereafter."

Hunter cleared his throat. She hadn't been scary. She'd been hot as hell. Trevor was a damn fool, and probably gay. Any red-blooded, heterosexual vampire would have fallen at her feet in a fit of lust. "The riding crop?"

"From the stables." Her eyes narrowed, and she looked away. "I should have hit him harder. I should have refused the blood exchange."

Hunter clamped down on the rampant physical response still plaguing him. "You can't look at what happened from that perspective, Phoebe."

"I'm looking at it from the perspective that it was a mistake from start to finish. Marriage, even vampire marriages, should be for the right reasons, and being a sacrifice for a cause, no matter how noble, is not one of them."

"Giving how long we live, I believe you're right."

Silence settled between them.

"We'd better go. Unless you want to check out Dreamland," Hunter said, with a nudge, a teasing gleam in his eye.

Phoebe's eyes narrowed and her jaw muscle rippled. "When I catch up with that butt-munching dingleberry, I'm going to crush him."

Chapter 9

JOHNSON'S PIT STOP huddled in the middle of a large parking lot. With its rusty tin roof and sagging steps leading up to the rough plank front porch, the structure looked ready to collapse at any moment.

Parked in front were five pickup trucks and a black SUV. Ancil, Hunter's assistant, was nowhere to be seen.

Aware of dawn creeping closer, Phoebe jumped out of the car. Though they made good time, she could feel the sun coming, and was anxious to get to the safety of the cabin.

Hunter fell in beside her as they approached the store. The screen door screeched a melodic introduction when they entered, interrupting the pool game in progress. Three of the four men standing at the table straightened and turned their attention toward the door. The strong, musky scent of wolf and bear lingered in the air.

"They're shifters," Hunter stated.

"Of course. The store's owned by Leonard and Clara Johnson, who are bear shifters. But they'll wait on us just like they would anyone else. After six at night, they open the bar in the back and do quite a booming business."

The interior of the store was nothing like the outside. Strong wooden beams crisscrossed the open roof, and the wide, planked floor stretched out of sight, pale gray and shiny clean. Metal shelves holding a selection of items organized with military precision ran in parallel rows and lined the walls on either side.

Phoebe sauntered around the small counter space topped by a cash register and moseyed down the wide middle aisle toward the pool table.

A slender man, who'd been hidden by the large bulk of the other three, straightened after making his shot. "Hey, Hunter." His dark eyes strayed to Phoebe and he smiled, showing human teeth.

"Hunter?" One of the shifters braced his feet and eyed Hunter with interest. He rested the thick end of his cue stick on the floor but kept the fingers of both hands wrapped around the narrow end. The shifter's shoulders were as wide as a doorway, his arms and legs thick with muscle.

"A man learns to live with the moniker his parents give him, Babe," Phoebe said in a soothing tone, and patted the big man's arm.

He continued to study Hunter, but finally tore his gaze away to look at her. "Ain't that the truth? But to keep the confusion down, he might want to go by his initials while he's in here. Anybody starts talking about hunters, the temperature drops and tempers rise."

Hunter nodded. "Understood." Hunter extended his

hand. "You can call me Sam."

The big shifter didn't say pleased to meet you, but he accepted the handshake.

Phoebe stepped in to do the introductions, since the three shifters and Hunter continued to do the sizing up things men of all ages and species seemed to want to do. "These are Shirley and Marian, Babe's brothers. They look out for the cabin when I'm not here."

Hunter nodded to the other two men. "That's very neighborly of you."

"Phoebe's been real kind to our mother. She took family photos of us just a few months back. Did a professional job of it, too."

Babe's attention swung back to Phoebe while the other two men eased up close to Hunter. "I drove by the cabin last evening, and musta just missed you, Phoebe. The lights were on, but nobody was there."

Phoebe controlled her expression with difficulty. If she said they hadn't been there, the three Bear shifters were so territorial and protective of the area, they would feel they needed to step in. It would put them at risk and drop them in the midst of a dangerous vampire situation. If something were to happen...

"We were out and about, guys. I've been showing Sam around. We'll just be staying one more day, then going back to Scryville." Someone at the house had to have fed Trevor information about the cabin. And it was the perfect place to hide. Isolated, yet protected. What were the odds they'd show up in time to discover him? If it was him.

"It's a shame. The deer are starting to shed their velvet. I know you wanted to get some pictures of them last summer."

"I didn't bring my camera."

Babe's bushy brows went up. "I didn't think you went anywhere without it."

"This was a spur-of-the-moment trip. Sam is new to the area, and wanted to see the mountains and the lake."

Babe's face lit up. "Hey, you were supposed to get married this week."

She'd hoped he'd forgotten about the wedding. How was she supposed to explain, getting married to one man and being here at the cabin with another? "Yeah. We did." She hooked an arm around Hunter's waist and leaned in against him. Hunter wrapped an arm around her waist and snuggled her up against his tall, muscular frame.

"Congrats. No wonder you were out. I suppose this is sort of a short honeymoon trip."

Hunter gave her a squeeze. "This is only the beginning. We may travel all over the state."

If Trevor had already left, they certainly might. If he was here, they'd get him. "It won't be dark much longer, and I'd like to go back to the cabin and settle in before sunrise," Phoebe said. "Ancil, if you can bring out those few things we forgot, you and the boys can get back to your pool game."

"They're just out in the car, Phoebe."

Ancil placed his cue stick diagonally across one corner of the table and led the way outside.

"I'm sorry." Phoebe turned to Hunter as soon as they were outside. "I couldn't think of any graceful way to explain..."

She started to withdraw, but Hunter caught her arm and held it. "It's all right, Phoebe. I understand how awkward this is for you. You know, I've never known a vampire who doesn't recognize the boundaries between each preternatural species. And you've not only managed to make friends, but they accept you without reserve."

"I don't see any difference between them and us, other than our eating habits."

Hunter's gray eyes darkened, and he leaned in to give her a slow, thorough kiss. She'd been breathing while she spoke, but now she couldn't seem to. A slow, tingling pulse of need built low in her belly and spread. When he drew back, regret flooded her.

Hunter looked over her shoulder toward the store. "Your friends are watching us, and we need to leave before they decide to join us."

Had he only been kissing her for show? Based on the flare of color she saw along his cheekbones, that would be a no. Or was it a trick of the lights in the parking lot?

Ancil lifted a large duffel bag and a small cooler out of the SUV and lugged them over. Hunter opened the trunk, and the man loaded the items inside.

"Shall I come with you?" Ancil asked.

"No. It's too dangerous. If this poison can affect us, it would be instantly lethal to you."

"You may need this, sir." Ancil lifted a pistol and holster out of the duffel bag and handed it to Hunter. "It may slow him down so you can capture him."

Phoebe was surprised when Hunter reached for the weapon and slipped the holster around his waist, adjusting it so the gun fit at the small of his back. She'd never seen a vampire use a firearm against other vampires. For the most part they fought hand-to-hand.

"I'll use whatever I have to give me an edge, Phoebe. You need to do the same."

She froze. He'd seen the video from the wedding, the fire. Was he suggesting she should use her gift if they confronted Trevor? Had he also felt the wave of power she projected while they were tracking him, as Zaira had? The short video hadn't shown her setting the others alight. But someone might have come forward with a more revealing video.

She needed to give Hunter that retainer right away.

HUNTER FOCUSED ON the road ahead. "You okay?" he asked in the face of Phoebe's continued silence.

"Yes. Just anxious to get there. Go left up ahead when

the road forks. You'll have to slow down. The road is very winding, and the house is extremely isolated. I'll tell you where to park so we can walk in and surprise them if they're still there."

Hunter glanced in her direction as the first lightening of the sky glowed up ahead. "I don't go down right away after sunup. If you feel yourself about to go, try to get to safety. I'll be okay on my own."

She was silent several moments. "Don't sacrifice yourself for me. But do whatever it takes to get the poison so they can make an antidote."

Hunter swallowed. He'd never met a woman like her before. She had the mind-set of the agents he worked with.

"You'll need to slow down," she said. "The road is on the left."

Hunter turned onto the gravel road.

"You can pull in behind some of this growth ahead, and leave the car on the right. There's nothing there to puncture a tire."

The brush on either side blended into tall wild mountain laurel and azaleas. He eased the car off the road behind the tallest of the bushes. The bottom scraped, but he ignored it. When he killed the engine, Phoebe laid a hand on his arm.

"The cabin has three levels. The basement level is the secure sleeping level for us. It's windowless, but has an escape hatch beneath the front porch, as well as at the back of the house. The first floor contains the living spaces of kitchen, living room, game room, library, and a bathroom. It's all open. The stairway goes up to the second floor from there, and goes down to the basement on the opposite side. The second floor is where the servant bedrooms are, but we rarely bring servants with us. Security is tight on the bottom floor. Reinforced steel doors and a keypad that requires a key card and a pin. I have them both."

Hunter gave her cold hand a squeeze. "Breathe, Phoebe."

A small smile peeked out at him. "I'm good."

"After this is over, we need to talk."

She glanced out toward the horizon. "When there's time."

"Yes." He shoved open the door.

Phoebe led the way through the thick forest, since she knew the way. Hunter placed his feet in her tracks so he would make as little noise as possible. After a five-minute walk, they came upon the house. The lights were on, and a green Jeep was parked in the drive. The log house, built on a tall, windowless rock foundation, huddled beneath the trees. If Trevor and his human servant were in there, he might have gone on to sleep and left the servant to stand watch.

"I'll go look in the windows to see if there's any movement inside." Hunter whispered against her ear.

"I'll take care of the vehicle."

If she was taking care of the car, she'd be out of range of attack, since the car was a short distance down the drive. He shot her a thumbs-up.

As soon as she broke away, Hunter sped to the porch and stopped outside the window next to the front door. He peered in, but saw no one in the great room. The floor plan was just as she'd described it and was easy to scope out. He could see from one end of the house to the back door. Nothing moved.

Phoebe sped up to join him. She took a small folding wallet out of her back pocket, extracted a key card, slid it through the scanner, typed in a number, and opened the door. It swung inward soundlessly.

Hunter brushed his fingertips against her wrist and flattened his other palm in a downward motion, giving her a stop-wait signal. They both froze and listened intently to the sounds inside the house. The refrigerator motor, though very quiet, overwhelmed any other sound.

He signaled upstairs and led the way. The house, though small, was exquisitely appointed, with beautiful hardwood floors and high-end fixtures. They searched the five bedrooms and bathrooms systematically. All were empty.

Time for the downstairs apartments. Hunter's lips almost brushed her ear. "Is the setup for the downstairs rooms the same as upstairs?"

"Yes. Except for the exits."

"Okay. Let's do this."

Phoebe used her key card again and keyed in her pin. The heavy steel door swung silently toward them. Lights automatically flicked on. A body lay just inside the stairwell, facedown.

Hunter bent to turn the man onto his back. His eyes stared blindly upward.

"That's Jed, Trevor's human servant. I met him at Arthur's house."

When Hunter tugged him free of the steps and lowered him onto the floor, the man's broken neck flopped like a wet noodle.

"Let's finish this," Hunter murmured, though the possibility of Trevor being here was becoming less and less likely.

Their systematic search confirmed his suspicion. When they stood just outside the last bedroom, Hunter could feel the sun coming, but Phoebe was already fading, and leaned against the wall for support.

"You didn't seem surprised to find Jed dead."

Phoebe's mouth flattened, but there was a flicker of regret in her expression as she glanced toward the stairs. "I'm not. Trevor has a penchant for threatening, torturing, and otherwise treating the servants cruelly when no one's watching."

Outrage as explosively charged as a blasting cap crackled through Hunter's body. "And your sire was going to give you to him?"

Phoebe looked away, her expression blank. "I'm not a servant, and he wasn't giving me to him. I wasn't going to live with him. I was leaving to live elsewhere as soon as the wedding was over."

"Where were you going?"

"I was going to come here for a short time, since I've purchased a house close by which is in the process of being renovated and made secure."

"Who else besides you and Arthur has a key card and the numbers to get into this house?"

"Luke has one as well, and I've given one to Babe, since he comes up to check the house and do repairs when they're needed."

"Well, we know Babe didn't open the house to Trevor and his man, since he thought it was you here. I can't imagine Arthur giving up the key. What about Luke?"

"Never. Someone had to have taken it." Her outraged tone didn't sound as certain as she probably wished. Phoebe's eyes widened, and she looked at him. "Hunter." The sun had risen. He saw shock and fear in her expression before her features went lax and she collapsed. He leapt forward and caught her.

He carried her into the only femininely decorated bedroom in the basement and placed her on the bed. He carefully straightened her limbs and brushed her colorful hair off her face. The exotic tilt of her eyes and the generous curve of her mouth drew his attention, but he tried not to think about that brief kiss they shared outside the Pit Stop earlier. It would be too voyeuristic to think about it while she was lying there, vulnerable and beautiful.

He wondered at that sudden look of shock and fear. He never feared his death, normally feeling annoyed or impatient about it instead. There were always things he had to leave unfinished when the need to sleep overcame him. Like now. But he needed to report to Vlad before seeking his own rest. He'd notify Stewart later, when he awoke again.

He shot off a quick text, notifying Vlad of the dead servant and their location. He climbed the stairs to secure the door, then returned to Phoebe's room and did the same. He'd be awake before she was, and she'd never know he slept beside her. And even if she did, he didn't care. That brief kiss more than warned her of his interest. And her response told him a lot in return.

He stretched out beside her, placed a hand over hers, and let himself go.

Chapter 10

P HOEBE AWOKE AS though she was moving from one
thought to the next. The anxiety of that last moment
before she slept still lingered. Why did it go down that way
every time? She turned onto her side and noticed the hollow
on the pillow next to her. Her entire body was electrified
with emotions, and her heart thundered.

Hunter had slept with her on her bed. Had she been able
to blush, she would have. She rolled to her feet to find the
bag of new clothes inside the door. She took it into the
bathroom to shower, emerging ten minutes later, refreshed
and ready for whatever might come next.

When she climbed the stairs, she found the metal door
cracked open, and no sign of a body on the floor.

Hearing voices in the kitchen, she followed the sound,
and came to a halt in the doorway. The two large, dark-
haired men standing on either side of the kitchen island
seemed to have been created from the same mold. Both
men's features were intensely masculine, almost hawk-like,
their physical presences mesmerizing.

Hunter noticed her first, and as soon as he did, the male

with him turned to look over his shoulder. His dark eyes focused on her with a predatory gleam, and his power reached out to her, brushing against her like a caress.

Phoebe threw up her own power, shoving aside the unwanted intrusion. Hunter leapt across the island to land between them, his gray eyes glowing blue and his fangs distended. The taut line of his body conveyed aggression as clearly as his clenched fists.

Phoebe's heart tripped at Hunter's show of protectiveness, concerned for him.

The strange male's brows shot up. "I meant no insult, my friend." The deep, husky voice said, with an unfamiliar accent.

"Hunter," Phoebe said as she sauntered forward and stood next to him. She wrapped her fingers lightly around his upper arm to find the bulky muscle there rock-hard with tension.

The stranger bent his head in an old-fashioned show of respect. "I am Vlad Tepes."

"Phoebe Stewart. Hunter has mentioned you."

"He has also mentioned you, Ms. Stewart." His laser eyes swept away to focus on Hunter. "But he did not tell me how special you are."

She studied his expression. "Special?"

"You are not just vampire."

Phoebe remained silent a moment. Her heart beat so she could feel her slow vampire blood rushing through her veins. "We all bring what gifts we have as humans with us when we become vampire."

"Not always."

Phoebe continued to gaze at him in silence.

Her phone rang, and she dragged it free of her back pocket, glad to see it was Arthur. "Excuse me." She moved away from Hunter and his sire.

"The local Vampire Council has asked to meet with you tonight," Arthur announced.

"Good. What time?" She wandered to the refrigerator and removed one of the packets of blood. She popped the plug out of the straw-like extension at the top of the plastic bag and sucked down the sweet-salty flavor of 0 negative, shivering at the immediate rush.

"They wish to meet at two o'clock this morning. Ricci will be coming as well."

"Okay." If the local Council figured out what she could do, there would be a price on her head. They were against anyone who had special gifts above what vampirism brought them.

Maybe Adcock would trip and fall on a sharp stake before the meeting. She could only hope.

"Why do you think Ricci has decided to come?"

"I don't know, my dear, but rumor has it things have gone south for him since the wedding. His business partners have decided he is not trustworthy."

"Well, duh."

Arthur chuckled. "Phoebe. After nearly sixty years you've still managed to retain that black and white, good or bad view of behavior, as though we're all human. Which we are not."

"Everyone is human, Arthur."

"I think I've just been insulted." He sounded more amused than upset.

"Vampirism just emphasizes the predatory qualities we all have. And we're more direct with our behavior because we recognize what we are. But humans are the true predators."

She continued, pacing and gesturing with her free hand. "They camouflage their true selves with a layer of civility. They've had a hundred and fifty thousand years to try and kill each other off, and everything else on the planet besides, and they're slowly and surely gaining on it. They've gotten more sophisticated with their weapons and their means of destruction, and eventually they'll manage to do it. We'll be nothing more than a footnote when we starve to death because they've managed to wipe themselves out."

"But I suggest you leave all this out of the meeting later," Arthur replied. "The Council is normally only interested in local politics, not the big picture."

Phoebe laughed. "All right. I promise not to wax philosophical about anything but that pompous, sniveling, cowardly asswipe who left me to be staked while he hid in the bushes." A quick wave of rage rushed through her. "Has anyone looked into his finances to see if he was paid off by Ricci or his people?"

"He wasn't paid. He's a coward, and cowards always have a heightened sense of self-preservation when it comes to saving their own worthless hides."

"I'll keep that in mind for next time. Perhaps I need to improve my aim."

"Now, now, my dear. We both know you are not a murderer."

"A girl can wish for a fatal accident, can't she?"

Arthur gave a bark of laughter. "Be here by one thirty."

"Okay, Arthur." She hung up and turned to find Vlad and Hunter had been listening to her every word. She smiled her most genteel hostess smile. "Would anyone else care for some blood?" She held up the partially emptied packet, pushed in the stopper, and laid it on the sink.

Vlad laughed. "You are delightful, my dear."

She didn't know whether to be pleased or not about his comment. Probably not.

"Where has Jeb gotten off to?" The poor, dead man couldn't very well get up and walk away, and he was nowhere in sight.

Hunter spoke for the first time since her appearance. "He has been returned to the Ricci clan for burial."

"Thank you for seeing to that. I think he was with Trevor for nearly ninety years. I can't imagine why Trevor would suddenly kill him. Do you think someone broke in, killed Jeb, and took Trevor? He does, after all, have a lethal weapon."

Hunter's dark brows forked in a frown. "We have just been debating that."

"Ricci will be at the Council meeting tonight. Perhaps you'll have time to speak with him, if you wish to attend." She looked to Hunter first, then to Vlad, including him in the invitation, though she wasn't sure about the wisdom having three powerful master vampires attending such a function.

"I believe I will leave it up to Hunter to learn what he can during the meeting. You will keep me informed, Hunter?"

"Of course."

Vlad approached her and extended his hand. Phoebe placed her fingers in his grasp. "It was very nice to meet you, Phoebe." He bowed over her hand.

"Thank you."

Vlad chuckled. "It is refreshing to see someone who is neither cowed nor overly impressed by power."

"Those who have true power don't have to wield it. The promise is enough, isn't it?"

"Indeed. And I believe you have true promise." He gave her hand a squeeze before moving so quickly her senses picked up only a brush of air against her skin, and he was gone.

She released her breath on a sigh and a shudder. "He's

scary as hell."

Hunter's eyes still glowed blue. "Yes, he is. He is also very impressed by you."

"I wasn't trying to impress him."

"He knew that as well." He ran his fingertips down her arm. "I have never moved to protect someone from him before."

"He could have hurt you."

"Yes. Easily."

She cupped his cheek and ran her thumb over his cheekbone. "Thank you for your protection." She had planned to secure his discretion with a retainer, but after his attempt to shield her from Vlad...it seemed unnecessary. "We need to get a move on. I'll pack my things."

"You need to finish your meal. You may need your strength during the meeting."

She wouldn't need her strength. She'd need patience and control to avoid barbecuing Adcock like a chicken wing.

Once they were on their way back to town, her thoughts returned to that concave depression in the pillow next to hers. "Thank you for taking care of me last night."

"You're welcome. It's been some time since I shared my sleep with someone. It was nice waking up to you."

A prickle of heat bathed her face. Was she actually blushing? How was that possible?

"We're not encouraged to get involved with our clients. But after this is over, Phoebe, I'd like for us to spend some time together."

If she lived. Emotion swamped her and made it hard to swallow. "It may be some time before I'm a free woman."

"No it won't." He shot her a glance. "There are several agencies who are very interested in Trevor and his poison. He'll be staked if they capture him."

Did Hunter's sire have a hand in that plan? "Is that what Vlad said?"

"Yes. Among other things. The house you're having remodeled, how secure is it?"

"We can drive by and see how close to finished they are. Turn to the left up here."

The road wound higher into the mountains. The highway, thickly lined with trees, allowed only a glimpse now and then of the half-moon. After another mile, she told him to turn to the left down a narrow, paved road.

The house was built of huge logs with a rock foundation. A wraparound porch with a tin roof encircled the first floor, while atop the second floor roof was a widow's walk.

"That's unusual."

"You can see the lake from here. I love sitting up there and soaking in the moonlight. I miss sunlight, and moonlight is the closest thing I can get to it. Would you like to go up and enjoy the view for a while?"

"Yes."

She keyed in the password to open the door and hit the switch inside to turn on the lights. The walls were sheetrocked inside to cover the logs, giving the impression the interior of the house was infused with light. Some of the new furniture she ordered had arrived, and the men had unwrapped the items and set them in place. It was time to choose some lamps and pillows.

The new gray-green kitchen cabinets coordinated perfectly with the veins of gold and green in the black granite countertops, and the stainless steel appliances reflected the glow of the pot lights overhead.

The hardwood floors gleamed with the finish the brothers had applied since she was here last.

"What does a vampire need with a kitchen?" Hunter asked.

"I can cook for my shifter, witch, and human friends. I even have a couple of pixie and fairy friends I can make mead for."

Hunter's grin jumpstarted her heart into a flurry of beats. He looked younger when he smiled, and sexy as hell. "You are very unusual, Phoebe."

She thought about Vlad's comment about her being "not just vampire." Sooner or later Hunter would discover what she was, but not yet.

"The setup is very similar to Arthur's house. My bedroom is in the basement, but I'm planning to have one of the upstairs rooms secured as well. One has a skylight." She caught his hand and drew him to the stairs. Stainless steel banisters supported glass inserts so the light could pass through.

In the upstairs bedroom, Hunter studied the skylight over the bed.

"You could have a shield set on a timer just to be safe," Hunter suggested.

"That's a good idea."

"Who's doing the work for you?"

"Babe and his brothers. They can build anything, and they can repair anything too, including cars. And now for my favorite part...the stairs to the widow's walk are at the end of this hall."

The spiral stairway led up to a small, sheltered door leading out onto the roof. Adirondack chairs and small tables were set up to look out toward the lake. Moonlight touched the wings of a flock of large geese as they flew overhead, honking loudly.

"I love it here."

"I can tell." Hunter placed an arm around her waist and leaned an arm on the railing. "If this is where you've always wanted to be, why didn't you tell Arthur Stewart and move up here?"

Phoebe remained silent for a moment. "When I first transitioned, I had some adjustment issues. It was very hard for me to maintain control, and I needed help accepting some of the changes. I still struggle with some of them. I couldn't go back home and tell my parents what happened, and it was especially hard not being able to see them or let them know I was okay. They're both gone now." The grief was still there to tighten her throat and make her eyes sting.

"Arthur gave me a job managing some of his business ventures, which helped enormously, because it forced me to focus. He took me under his wing, became like a father to me. And Luke became a big brother."

She turned to look up at him. "Vlad was right. I'm not completely vampire. There's still a part of me that's more human than vamp." She couldn't reveal her every secret, but she wanted to trust him. "It's both a torment and a comfort still having these human feelings, hopes and dreams. I still miss feeling the sunlight on my skin. I still crave a good cheeseburger. Still want a home and family."

"Being a vampire doesn't mean you can't have a home. But allowing someone to control you usually does."

She noticed he didn't say family. "Vlad doesn't...control you?"

"No. I take the cases I'm interested in. I run my own life."

She remained silent for a moment. "I went along with the marriage because I thought if I did this one last thing for Arthur, I would have fulfilled my last obligation, and I could walk away."

"You're a powerful female, Phoebe. Why allow him to dominate you?"

She shook her head. "It isn't exactly like that. It's more like having a parent who depends on you, and you don't want to disappoint them. I owe him my life. One of his younger vamps attacked me and left me to die. Arthur turned me, then mentored me until I had some control."

"Did he turn you to save your life, or because he sensed you had other powers?"

She grimaced. He saw more than she wanted him to. She felt almost embarrassed having her every secret exposed. "I'm not naïve, I know why he turned me. But he's protected me, too. I care about him. Relationships can be so confusing and complicated."

Hunter's features hardened. "There's a fine line between protection and manipulation. He didn't do so well at the wedding, did he?"

"I didn't either."

"You still protected him, even though you almost died."

"It wasn't entirely altruistic, you know. Had he died, I'd have died, too. And others. That's what Trevor planned."

"But Luke wouldn't have died. Arthur didn't turn him. Could he be involved?"

"No. He wasn't at the house. He was holding the hand of a very rich, nervous vampire whose especially large clan was threatening to leave our area."

"What better alibi than to be gone? And it was a very important day for him to be gone."

"I told him to go, because it wasn't an important day to me. It was just something to get through."

"An even better reason for him to be there to support

you."

She remembered the phone call she overheard in the library, but pushed the memory away. Luke was her brother in every way. He would never hurt her. "What are you trying to do, Hunter?"

"It pisses me off that you're alone through all of this. The two most important people in your life aren't doing a damn thing to support or protect you."

It was true. But it was partly her fault. She began pushing them away long before the wedding. She'd become dissatisfied with her position in Arthur's business. Dissatisfied with her life. What was the point of living forever if she couldn't pursue her own passions?

What if it was too late?

Hunter cupped her face and kissed her softly, carefully, offering her comfort.

Phoebe's body went weak with sensation, and it didn't have a thing to do with the poison. She leaned into him and felt the response of his body to hers. Her lips parted and his tongue found hers. She moaned beneath the pressure of the kiss.

He raised his head and brushed his lips along her cheekbone. "You deserve better, Phoebe."

"Better than that?"

His smile flashed white in the dark. "We can work on it." He slid a warm hand down her back and pulled her in closer. "But you know what I'm saying."

"I'm moving in here as soon as this is over. That will make it better."

"Do you think so? You'll be isolated up here."

"But I'll be following my own passions instead of someone else's."

"That sounds promising." He gave her waist a squeeze. "And what kind of passions are we talking about?"

"I'm working on a series of low light photographs using a night vision photography system."

His brows rose. "You were a professional photographer?"

"Yes. I was at the wedding taking pictures when I was attacked and turned. It's taken me a long time to get back to it. Since I can't take photos in natural light...I've had to wait for technology to catch up to my needs."

"That's fantastic, Phoebe." He rested his forehead against hers. "You're going to do something special with your passion."

She smiled. "Yeah, I am, and maybe with a few others, too." She rose on tiptoe to capture his mouth in a long, thorough kiss.

"Damn shame we don't have time to pursue a few of those passions right now," he complained. With a sigh that was too heartfelt to be fake, he released her. "We'll make up for it later."

✧   ✧   ✧

POWER CRACKLED IN the air like static electricity. Only Arthur Stewart's master vampire influence kept the meeting from exploding.

Hunter scanned the group of black-clad Council members. The hunched, long-necked Adcock was exactly as Phoebe had described him—an old buzzard. And now Hunter had that apt image trapped in his head.

Arthur greeted yet another witness. His household had opened the ballroom at the house and, as usual, were treating the meeting like a social event. Because of the risk of poison, attendees were warned ahead of time that it was BYOB (bring your own blood). Snacks were optional in case someone wanted to bring a live donor.

As a species, vampires were nosy, and thrived on gossip. The marriage of Arthur Stewart's daughter and Ricci's son had been the main subject for weeks. Since the groom attempted murder only moments after the "I do's," it opened the entire event, plus its aftermath, up for endless speculation.

Specifically, Hunter had heard debates about what Phoebe might have done to deserve being attacked.

As if anyone deserved that.

Ricci arrived, and Hunter did a double-take when he saw him. He met the powerful, influential vampire nearly six months earlier, at a meeting of the National Council, but now his prosperously plump figure had shrunk, he had dark bladders beneath his eyes, as though he hadn't slept in weeks. He crept along like an old man, as though every step required all his concentration.

Arthur Stewart approached the master vampire and beckoned to Hunter to join them.

"Armanno, this is Hunter Knox."

Ricci nodded. "I have been made aware of your search for Trevor, Mr. Knox. My people and I are at your disposal to help in any way we can."

Hunter studied the man's paper white face. "You were not as cooperative a week ago, Master Ricci."

"I know. But since the wedding, several things have occurred. One of our most trusted human servants has been murdered, and several other members of our household have been poisoned, including myself. Two have already died. If we don't find Trevor soon, I will die, and take all the vampires in my line with me. And Trevor will take over the Ricci Clan."

"I assume you have people out hunting for Trevor," Hunter said.

"Yes. Of course."

Phoebe entered the room, and the noise levels and gossip increased. Dressed in a soft green shift and leggings, she'd covered the puncture wounds in her neck and the bruise—which were worsening again—with a silk scarf. She appeared feminine and fragile.

Hunter beckoned for Phoebe to join them, and as soon as she saw Ricci her features went taut. "Master Ricci. You do not look as hearty as you did a week ago."

"No, I am not, Phoebe. I fear I, too, have fallen victim to my son's avarice. Our blood supply was contaminated, and several of my people have been poisoned."

Phoebe remained silent a moment. "I'm very sorry, Signor Ricci."

Ricci grimaced. "You and your father are more generous than I deserve, Phoebe. I have brought several doses of the antidote with me. It does not work completely, but it may hold the poison at bay long enough for the scientists you have employed to find a lasting cure."

How the hell had Ricci heard about that? "It will be impossible to find a lasting antidote unless we have an undiluted sample of the poison, Signor Ricci," Hunter explained.

Ricci shook his head with a sigh. "Only Trevor knows the person responsible for the poison. Only he has a full-strength sample of the compound."

"We are hunting for him." Phoebe said softly. "But in the meantime, I don't intend to allow him to gain control of our clan. I expect you to stand with me on that before the Council."

"Yes. Of course."

She stepped very close to Ricci, her eyes glowing like green fire. "I do not intend to claim your clan, no matter what happens, Signor Ricci. But I will make you a promise. Should you die before me, I will make it my calling in life to end Trevor. There are those of us who understand loyalty, and a son who would turn on his father doesn't deserve to benefit from his treachery."

Phoebe's deep sense of loyalty had kept her by Arthur Stewart's side, even though she was restless and unhappy, and now she extended that loyalty to a competing clan. Hunter could only admire her more.

It must have impressed Ricci too, because his Adam's apple bobbed as he swallowed. "Thank you."

Arthur clapped his hands to get everyone's attention. "If everyone will take a seat, we will begin the meeting."

The six Council member vampires, their dark evening clothes increasing the solemnity of the gathering, sat at a table at the front of the room. The group of twenty-five witnesses wandered to the five round tables and sat down.

The sudden increase of power resonating in the room upped Hunter's vigilance. Should violence erupt, it would be up to him and Luke Stewart to end it.

He watched Luke while he made one last sweep of the room, on alert to trouble. He'd wondered at Luke's relationship with Phoebe until he caught them doing rock, paper, scissors to decide who got to control the video they meant to show the Council.

"Good evening, everyone, and welcome to our illustrious Council members," Arthur began. "You are all aware of the purpose of this meeting. There has been some speculation regarding what actually happened during the wedding of my daughter Phoebe to Ricci's son Trevor last week.

"To that end, we have invited several guests who were present to testify as to what they saw, and we will show a video that will clarify those events—in particular, the behavior of my daughter's fiancé's right after the vows, as well as the behavior of a sitting Council member, who is sworn to protect and uphold the civilized behavior among clans."

"Luke, if you will dim the lights for us, we will all view the video together."

"Wait," Councilman Adcock rose to his feet. "I don't see what purpose viewing this will serve, since I believe it might have been edited to show a biased view of the events."

Arthur rose. "You have my word the video has not been tampered with, Councilman Adcock. It will be shown exactly as it was recorded. Or are you calling me a liar?"

"Does it show your daughter Phoebe starting the fire?"

"Yes." Luke said. "It shows her rolling a candle toward the Ricci clan while Trevor leapt off the platform and stalked toward my father with a stake. It also shows you standing behind him while he threatened my sister with said stake, and your hasty departure from the platform and disappearance into the woods when she needed help. Your cowardice could have cost my sister her life, and my father his as well."

Luke hit the button and the large screen on the wall came to life.

Hunter, though he'd seen the footage earlier, could not

take his eyes off Phoebe's image while she sauntered across the platform, all graceful and sexy. He hardened just watching her. When she leaned forward and daintily struck Trevor's neck, he wanted to leap at the screen.

Her lips were pink with Trevor's blood when she straightened, then tilted back onto the tall heels of her boots while she clawed at her throat. Seconds later she staggered and fell heavily to the platform.

Hunter glanced in Phoebe's direction to catch her looking away from the screen, her expression carefully blank. He turned back to see Trevor rip loose a part of the trellis and stalk toward her.

Adcock beat a hasty retreat off the platform, his black robe flapping around him like buzzard wings.

Just when Trevor was poised to plunge the stake into Phoebe's chest, a young male vampire leaped from the side and drove him back. Trevor twisted the vampire's arm, breaking it as he slung him forward, and the male tumbled over Phoebe and into the nest of Ricci vampires. Trevor then stalked off the platform, the stake in his hand and his focus on Arthur Stewart.

A candle toppled off one of the tall candelabras on the platform while Phoebe's weak struggles to roll onto her side were partially obscured because of the camera angle. Then a rolling ball of light tumbled across the floor toward one of the Ricci vampires. The male went up like fireworks, his screams silent and horrifying. The fire leaped from vampire to vampire, consuming them like they were paper dolls, while the swirling blaze spiraled into the sky, towering above the scattering crowd of vampires.

Ricci tumbled to the ground. Arthur caught something Ricci tossed to him and stalked to the platform to lift Phoebe into a sitting position. He tipped something between her parted lips.

The fire died suddenly, leaving a blackened trail of ash and burned grass across the lawn. The suddenness of Phoebe's death never failed to grab Hunter's heart.

And she'd been very close to permanent death for nearly twenty-four hours.

He turned to look at Phoebe, then Adcock and Ricci.

"Do we need to replay your part in this, Adcock?" Luke asked. "Or should we discuss the part you should have, but didn't, play?"

The six Council members were looking everywhere but at the company of vampires surrounding them.

One of the Council members sitting next to Adcock rose. "What do you want from us?"

Arthur rose. "We want the marriage between my daughter and Trevor Ricci dissolved, and the contract Armanno Ricci and I signed declared null and void. Or would you rather take the chance of something happening to all of us"—Arthur gestured around him "—and ending up answering to Trevor?"

"No, we would not want that."

"There may be a problem dissolving the marriage, Master Stewart," Adcock said, his gaze upon the ground, though he spoke to Arthur.

"What sort of problem?" Phoebe asked.

"It usually takes the presence of both parties before us to deny a marriage."

"Is attempted murder not sufficient grounds for divorce? Or, better yet, since the marriage was not consummated, why can we not annul it?"

"It is written in our law that the bond has to be at least six months long before it can be dissolved. To give it a chance."

"I may not be alive in six months, Adcock."

"Something that is always true for all of us."

Irritation at the vampire's arrogance gripped Hunter by the back of the neck and squeezed. He fought the urge to snatch him out of his chair and shake him till his neck snapped.

"I will not die Trevor Ricci's wife." There was a predatory grace in the way Phoebe moved toward Adcock, her eyes glowing with an eerie light. Hunter moved to cut her off before she reached the Councilman. "Move, Hunter. I do not mean to kill him."

"If you harm him, you may never find a way to annul the marriage, Phoebe."

She lifted her hand gracefully...and a force jerked him out of her way and set him down twenty feet away with a jolt.

She returned her attention to Adcock. "We both know the reason you ran during the fight. You are a coward, and your life means more to you than anyone else's. I don't hold that against you. But I will give you an incentive to solve this problem...

"For every day I must wait for this marriage to be dissolved, you will feel pain. For every day you have found no way to make it possible, the pain will worsen. When you find a way to break it and come to me with it, your pain will end." She twirled her finger around and around, stirring the air while her face glowed with an inner power. A pain/pleasure flow of electricity sizzled along Hunter's skin, even from twenty feet away.

The Vampire Council members moved restlessly, their robes rustling as though stirred by a warm wind.

Hunter suddenly understood what his sire meant when he said she had promise. Phoebe Stewart was possibly the second most powerful vampire he had ever met.

"If I die before you find the solution, you will live with this pain forever."

Adcock caught his breath and gripped his chest. "You can't do this."

Phoebe's features hardened into a mask. "I already have. I suggest you and your other Council members find a solution for the dissolution of both the marriage and my father's contract immediately." Her scornful look raked the

Council, and they shrank away from her. "Otherwise I may have to create an incentive that will inspire you all."

✧　✧　✧

PHOEBE STALKED OUT of the ballroom, too angry to maintain the façade of control. She needed to escape this house and get as far away from Adcock as possible. Otherwise she might do something she'd regret. His arrogance knew no bounds, and he'd earned his punishment.

The fact that she truly might be dead before they found Trevor and the poison didn't matter to him. He was a typical vampire, in that death had dulled his ability to feel empathy or caring for anyone but himself.

She hoped she never lost the ability to feel, no matter how much it hurt. And she was hurting plenty right now.

She hurried up the stairs to the gallery and rushed to her bedroom. When she pulled aside the scarf, she saw the puncture wounds were once again draining. The bite was getting worse by the moment. After only two days, her body had finally decided it could no longer heal the wound, and the bite was throbbing again. She threw the last of the casual travel clothes she'd set out into her suitcase, tossed the spike heels she'd worn to attend the meeting into the closet, and got out a soft pair of flats.

"May we come in, Phoebe?" Arthur asked from the doorway. Hunter and Luke stood next to him.

"This is your house, Arthur. You can enter any room

you wish."

"Where do you plan to go, Phoebe?" Arthur asked.

"Away."

"This is your home."

"No it isn't. Not anymore. I cannot trust the people or the vampires in this house any longer. And I cannot trust myself to deal with them reasonably."

"That includes me?" Arthur asked.

For the second time since she'd become a vampire, she felt nauseous. "Yes, it includes you, Arthur. I'm no longer part of your corporation. Which makes me a free agent, and I can do whatever I damn well please now." She zipped her suitcase.

"Even if I order you to remain here."

"You don't want to do that, Arthur." She went to the three poster-sized photos she so often sat before to calm herself, taking them off the wall to stack them next to the suitcase.

"We need to talk, Phoebe." Arthur said in his most conciliatory tone. "There are things you need to know."

She shook her head. "You used me to deal with Trevor and Armanno before the wedding. And you used me to deal with the Council just now. You expected me to kill Trevor and Armanno. Did you honestly believe I didn't know what your plans were? Whenever you decide it's time to apply brute force, you use me. I am tired of being used. I'm trapped in this damnable marriage to a male I detest because you wanted to use me for that, too. What more do I need to know?"

"If you had told me …"

"I was going to leave right after the wedding, Arthur. I thought it would be a marriage in name only. After all, since vampires don't give a shit about the ideals of loyalty, marriage, the sanctity of life, why would it have been anything else?"

Phoebe tucked the poster-sized photos under her arm and gripped her suitcase. "I wish you'd never turned me. I was never meant to be a vampire. You should have let me die. And now I don't have very much time left, I don't want to spend it here. I want to go to my own home, the home I've been building in the mountains, and live out what time I have left the way I want."

Hunter stepped in front of her. "Phoebe, you're at your most vulnerable right now. You will be isolated there, unprotected."

"What difference does that make to anyone but me, Hunter?"

His gray eyes looked more intense than she'd ever seen them. "It makes a difference to me."

"What you're feeling won't last. Male vampires aren't capable of fidelity for any length of time. There's too much more to experience out there. And too much time to do so."

She felt an overwhelming need to weep and shoved past him, zipping out of the room with vampire speed before

Luke could stop her.

✧   ✧   ✧

"SHE HAS EVERY right to be angry. Everything she said is true. You had to have known what kind of male you were giving her to," Hunter snapped. "Did you plan for her to kill him so you could gain control of the Southeastern territory?"

"There are other issues you are not aware of, Hunter. It was important for her to be in the midst of the Ricci clan. Recently key leaders have been killed. Angelina Gomez in Texas was killed, and it nearly decimated the vampire population there. Andre Cassard fell in Louisiana, and the Creoles have been halved."

"You should have told her why she needed to be there. She's your daughter. She's been loyal to you since her transition. And with her power, you've probably been using her to your advantage for years. But she needed to know why. Not to be thrust into it blindly."

"It has been a balancing act, Hunter. She is very power-ful. Do you know what the Security Council might do to her if they discover what she can do?"

"But you were going to use her as an assassin anyway, weren't you?"

"I knew she would protect herself when the time came."

"But she didn't. She protected you instead."

Arthur flinched. "I know she did. With her last strength. For those last few minutes I thought she had died and…" His eyes flared with pain. "Whatever you may think, I love my daughter."

Hunter attempted to control his outrage. "You didn't tell her you were on a fishing expedition. You didn't prepare her for any of this. She thinks you wanted to get rid of her."

"Never. I was going to lay it all out for her before she left. She is not good at hiding her feelings, and I was concerned that if I told her everything beforehand she might do something to make Ricci and Trevor suspicious. At least her disinterest in Trevor kept him off balance."

"So you were manipulating her to your own ends. For all her strengths as a vampire, she still thinks like a human, with human emotions, human values. She recognized Trevor's deliberate cruelty and didn't trust herself not to react to it. She was going to leave right after the ceremony because she knew she would kill him eventually. She has killed, but she doesn't enjoy it like some.

"As for the Vampire Council, Vlad met with her for only ten minutes and recognized how powerful she is. She hides it well, but he is good at sensing things. Hell, I sensed it, but didn't know the half of it. I still don't."

Arthur fisted his hands. "You have to go after her. Make certain she is safe. Trevor won't rest until he ends her, because he needs her dead so he can get to me. Luke and I have discovered who was responsible for Phoebe's blood supply being compromised, and he has been cultivating the woman's interest for some time."

Hunter jerked around to face Luke. "Does this female have the poison?"

Luke nodded. "We believe she does. I believe she has been working for Ricci and Trevor from the beginning."

"Why the hell haven't you taken her?"

Luke and Arthur exchanged a glance. "We were hoping to use her to bring Trevor in."

By the blood of the Goddess! They were going to let Phoebe die. "If she wasn't as strong as she is, Phoebe would already be dead. Did you not notice the bruise is expanding again, and her scarf was sticking to the wound?"

"Should Trevor discover she's alone, he'll come after her," Luke said, his features alive with concern.

At least her brother was truly concerned for her. An idea struck him. Hunter hesitated. "Her isolation would not necessarily be a bad thing under the right circumstances. Can you feed this woman Phoebe's location?"

"You'd use Phoebe as bait?" Luke shook his head.

If he used her as Arthur had done so many times before... "Not without her knowledge. I'll catch up to her and call you to let you know whether she agrees or not."

Arthur nodded. "Hurry."

Chapter 11

Dizziness hit Phoebe, and she pulled her cherry red Mustang off the side of the road and rested her head on steering wheel. Nausea rolled over her, and she swallowed against the urge to vomit, shaking with a combination of chills and weakness. Perhaps if Zaira could give her another healing treatment...

She shouldn't have spoken to Arthur the way she did. But she wasn't going to apologize. He had never even apologized for getting her entangled in this Trevor fiasco. She was so angry with him. Angry with Adcock. Angry with everything. And angry with herself for wasting so much time when she could have been living her life the way she wanted to, instead of the way someone else dictated. She should have tried harder to break away. She should have grown a pair and told Arthur long ago how she felt.

Eventually her stomach quit tumbling enough that she could assess how she was feeling. There were a couple of bags of blood at the house. She'd feel better once she drank one of them. She just had to get there.

She glanced around to make sure the road was clear and

started to pull out. Her car's wheels moved but the vehicle didn't. She jerked her attention forward to find Hunter with his hands braced on the grill, holding the vehicle in place. She lifted her foot off the gas pedal, threw the car into park, jerked her seatbelt free, and opened the door.

"What are you doing?"

Hunter's eyes glowed with a blue gray light. "You can't go off alone, Phoebe. And you can't expect me to stay behind if you do."

"Where's your car?"

"I didn't need one to catch up to you. The Hamiltons and Babe and his brothers are going to meet us at your house."

"Why?"

"Because Luke is going to feed the info of your location to Sophia. He has suspected her of being in cahoots with Ricci and Trevor for quite a while, and he's pretty sure she's the one who laced your food with the poison. They'll watch her to try and catch her in the act, and then take her down. But it also means Trevor may come for you. You'll be our bait if you agree to it."

"This is what Arthur wanted to talk to me about?"

"No. He was trying to apologize to you. But it was the plan we came up with after you left."

Tears burned her eyes and the anger drained out of her. "Of course I'm okay with it."

"While I drive, phone Arthur and tell him. He's waiting

for my call, but he'll be happier to hear it from you."

She reached for her cell phone in the cup holder between the seats, and was already hitting the number as she went around to get into the passenger seat.

Aware of Hunter listening to every word, Phoebe attempted to keep her emotions under control, but she was still a little tearful when she hung up.

Hunter covered her hands, clenched in her lap, with one of his own. "You need to feed, Phoebe," he said, offering his wrist to her.

"Hunter…" The idea of tasting his blood had other longings flaring to life. Her body ached with needs so long unfulfilled. How could she feel like this about him and at the same time feel so ill because of the poison?

"Drink, Phoebe. You'll need your strength in case we're attacked along the way."

Which was true enough. Her heart was thundering while she gripped his arm with both hands and lifted his wrist to her mouth. "I can give you pleasure while I feed, Hunter, beyond the sharing of blood. Would you like me to do that?"

His gray eyes heated and began to glow. His throat worked when he swallowed. "We don't have time."

"There's always time for pleasure." Her fangs distended, and she struck gently and sucked. The rush of tasting his blood sent a burst of adrenaline through her system. Her power reached out to him, as intimate as running her hands over him, caressing him, sparking his power in return.

"Phoebe—" He said her name on a breath.

She had to be careful not to take too much, but he tasted so good. Afraid she'd lose control, she licked the puncture wounds to close them and leaned over the console to cup his face in her hands and take his mouth in a kiss, ardent and hungry.

Hunter's hands slipped up under her top to cup her breast, kneading her flesh with careful pressure. She wanted him with a compulsion she'd never experienced before, and her power flared, bathing them both in sensual heat.

Hearing a sharp tap on the window behind him, Hunter broke away. A uniform shirt and the belt buckle of a police utility belt were all Phoebe could see. She covered her mouth to hold back a laugh.

"Busted," Hunter murmured and shot her a smile. He turned to look up at the man through the window.

The officer made a cranking motion and Hunter turned the ignition key and rolled down the window. "Good evening, officer."

"You've picked a bad spot to pull over and make out, sir."

Phoebe snorted. Hunter shot her a grin, followed by a look of warning.

The police officer leaned down and shined his flashlight into the car. "Miss Stewart, I didn't realize it was you."

"Caught red-handed." Phoebe laughed again. "Well, not

quite…"

Hunter tried to keep a straight face, though his shoulders shook with silent laughter.

"It was all my fault, Officer Howard," she continued.

The officer's lips twitched in an almost-smile.

"I pulled off the side of the road because I was feeling a little woozy. I've been a little under the weather. Hunter came to rescue me, and it's so late… I was just…thanking him."

"I see." He raised a dark brow. "My suggestion would be to hold off on the thank-yous until you get home, Miss Stewart."

She offered him her best kittenish smile. "I'll try to control myself, I promise."

That earned her a grin from both Hunter and Officer Howard.

"You'd better move along then…so you won't be tempted." The police officer touched the brim of his hat. "Have a good evening."

Hunter pulled the Mustang back on the road. "I've never been flagged by a cop for making out in a car." His gaze swept her face in the glow of the dashboard lights. "And I've never wanted anyone as much as I want you, Phoebe."

Her breath stopped and her heart raced. "I feel it too."

"Were you really woozy?"

"Yes."

He scowled in concern. "Feeling better now?"

"Yes."

"Luke and Arthur believe Sophia has the poison. As soon as they've found it, they'll rush it to the lab so the scientists can create an antidote."

"They need to hurry, Hunter."

His mouth cramped into a thin, firm line. "They know."

✧　✧　✧

HUNTER'S EYES FLEW open as soon as the sun set to find Phoebe lying beside him.

The sleep shirt covered her from neck to knees, and wasn't the least bit sexy. But it didn't matter. He still felt a rampant surge of need as soon as he looked at her. Could he wake her with a touch? His study halted at the bandage around her throat, which was stained along the edge. His stomach tightened.

He ran a fingertip along her cheek and sent a gentle trail of power along her skin.

Her eyes opened and she drew a deep breath. "Hunter?"

"Yes."

"What time is it?"

"Seven-thirty."

"I'm awake," she murmured drowsily and turned to nestle against him.

"Yeah. You need to feed, Phoebe."

She remained silent, and for a moment he thought she had fallen asleep again.

"Yeah. I need to feed." Her voice sounded breathy and weak.

"I'll get you something." Hunter slipped out from beneath her and knelt beside the small refrigerator next to the bed. He removed a packet of blood and got back into bed with her, lifting her easily against his bare chest and handing her the packet of blood.

She sipped the blood and cuddled close. He breathed in her orange blossom scent. "Have you ever been in love, Hunter?"

"Yes."

"How long did it last?"

"Nearly fifty years."

She tipped her head back to look up at him. "What happened?"

"It was nineteen-twenty. Travel back then was very difficult, and we rented a train car to go west to California. The men who worked on the trains were paid very little. When they opened the car and saw the two coffins, they decided to open them. They stripped Blythe of her jewelry, which wouldn't have been an issue, but they left the coffin lid up and the car door open as well. When the sun rose high enough, it lanced into the car, and she caught fire and burned to death, setting the car on fire.

"One of the men on board the train was Ancil. He and two other men put the fire out. When I awoke, I compelled him to tell me who the men were who had done it. I was mad with grief and rage, and I killed them."

"I'm so sorry, Hunter." Her tears were warm against his skin.

But the pain still throbbed deep within him. The horror of waking to Blythe's smoldering body, the remembered stench of her burned flesh, clamped a fist around his throat. He swallowed. "It was many years ago, Phoebe."

"That doesn't matter, does it? You still remember her, still grieve her loss. And after being together fifty years... You were so fortunate to find her."

"I was." He smoothed her hair and rested his cheek against it.

"I've never had that. The males I've dated only wanted a few weeks. They're either power-hungry or hungry for everything, like Trevor is."

He'd kill for a few weeks to know her. She was human enough that every experience seemed like something new. Like the police stop last night. He smiled just thinking about it.

But he could feel a definite ebb in her power. The poison was winning. His arms tightened around her. "It is their loss, Phoebe."

She rubbed her cheek against his bare chest, and he had his usual reaction, stone-hard in an instant.

"You'd think I'd learn to be more like them. Or at least behave more like them so I can blend in."

"I'm glad you're just you, Phoebe. You've taken the best

parts of your human self and blended them with your vampire. Most of us have lost the memory of what it's like to be human. But that doesn't mean we don't feel strongly. Perhaps the males you've dated haven't been mature enough."

"How old does a vampire have to be before he's mature enough?" she asked.

"A couple hundred years at least."

She handed him the empty blood packet and tilted her head to look up at him again. "How old are you?"

"Three hundred and two in vampire years. Three hundred and thirty in all."

"Can you walk in the sun?"

"Yes, I can."

"I want to walk in the sun, Hunter."

Something in her expression seized his throat with emotion. "You'll be able to in a few more years."

She laid her head against his shoulder. "Will you bathe with me?"

He swallowed. "If it's what you want, Phoebe."

"It is." She slipped out of bed and into the bathroom. He heard water running.

Sharing the bathroom with her while she brushed her teeth triggered a smile. How could brushing teeth seem sexy? She twisted her hair up at the crown of her head and clipped it with a comb. He brushed his teeth while she shed her nightshirt and lacy thong.

She was as slim as a willow branch, but muscular, like a runner. Her breasts seemed disproportionate to the rest of her, generous, the nipples pale pink beads.

He tossed his toothbrush aside, rinsed his mouth, and was there in a second to run a questing hand down the graceful curve of her spine, her skin like silk beneath his touch. He trailed a kiss across her shoulder to the back of her neck, and she shivered and reached back to grip his thigh and urge him closer.

He hardened even more. "You need to conserve your strength," he murmured against her ear. He slipped free of his sleep pants and stepped over the edge of the tub, settling into the waist-deep water to lean back against the tub.

She stepped over the side, lowered herself between his thighs, and leaned back against him.

Hunter eased her up into a sitting position before squirting some body wash into his palm and running his soapy hands over her back, shoulders, and the base of her neck, massaging as well as bathing her. The warm water trickled down in rivulets while he squeezed a loofah over her shoulders to rinse her skin.

WHEN HE DREW her back against him, Phoebe rested her head against his shoulder and felt the heat of his erection against the cheek of her ass. Her breathing grew unsteady.

Had she ever been treated with such tenderness? Never

by a male vampire. She'd wished for a sex toy while waiting to marry Trevor, but this was so much better. Was it because Hunter had been with someone for so long, and understood what it meant to be a mate?

When he soaped her breasts, her nipples puckered and a needy emptiness settled deep inside her. She covered his hands with her own. "Thank you for giving me this, Hunter."

His voice sounded husky. "Thank you for sharing it with me." He pressed an open-mouthed kiss against her shoulder. She ached for him to bite her, but the weakness reminded her of the danger. She turned her head to offer her mouth instead. His lips covered hers in an awkward, fervid kiss, their tongues tangling. She moaned beneath the intensity, and turned to rise on her knees and face him, pressing her soapy breasts against his chest.

She kissed him and teased his tongue into her mouth, sucking on it, and driving her need higher while making him hum. He cupped her wet buttocks and squeezed.

"We're supposed to be getting clean" he murmured against her lips.

She closed her eyes against a wave of dizziness and rubbed her cheek against his beard-stubbled one. "We are. I'm sharing my soap with you." She wiggled against him, and prayed the wooziness would pass.

Hunters ran his hands up and down the backs of her legs. She reached for the body wash and squirted some into her hands, working it over his broad shoulders and muscular arms, then rinsing the soap off them both with the loofah.

"I think we're clean enough, don't you?" he asked, cupping her breasts while he nibbled her earlobe and his breath fanned her neck. Delightful shivers trailed down her spine, and her breasts felt full and tight beneath his touch.

"Yes." She cupped his face and guided his mouth to hers. Her power wrapped around them and lifted them out of the water and onto their feet.

His impressive erection pressed against her belly. She cupped it and explored its length and thickness. Hunter's gray gaze glowed blue as his power flared and enveloped her in warmth. He lifted her easily, and she wrapped her legs around his waist.

The trip between tub and bed took but a second, and she held onto him while he crawled up on the bed. She lay back to gaze up into his face. "There are real perks to having vampire skills sometimes."

He chuckled. "And strength."

He removed the comb from her hair and ran his fingers through the shoulder-length locks, his power intensifying and spreading like static electricity over her skin. She caught her breath at the sensation and ran her hands up his chest. Then she forked her fingers through the dark hair at the back of his head and tugged his mouth back to hers.

Their lips clung, and their tongues meshed in a kiss that had her rolling her hips against him, inviting a deeper intimacy. He nipped at her shoulder without breaking the skin, then slid lower to take one nipple into his mouth to suck, then the other.

She caressed his neck and shoulders and let her power flow over him in a caress. He looked up at her, his eyes aglow, his fangs lengthening. "I want to bite you every time you do that...among other things."

His hand trailed over her belly and lower. He tempted her with his fingers and she bowed her back. His name emerged somewhere between a plea and a prayer.

He rose over her, and with a slow, scorching thrust, he was inside her, filling her, caressing her inside and out.

The act was so human, but Hunter's power seemed to meld with hers so every part of their beings seemed to touch. For a moment she struggled against it, trapped between fear for herself and fear for him. If she bonded too closely to him and died... Or worse, what if she set something on fire?

"It's okay, Phoebe. Let go," Hunter murmured above her while he quickened his slow, steady pace. Looking up into his face, she believed it would be...or was she befuddled by need or the beginnings of something more?

"Feed from my power." No male had ever invited her to do so. With Hunter moving inside her, stroking her in just the right spot, it was impossible not to want to reach for that wonderful strength. The sensations built to an unbearable peak, and his power flowed over her, through her, tearing away her resistance.

It was like riding a wave toward the unknown. Every inch of her body ached with titillating need, and the tension sharpened until she writhed beneath him, gasping and moaning.

Their power bloomed until they were locked inside a bubble of incomparable pleasure. Fulfillment rushed up and over her, and they flew over the edge together. It was then she opened herself and drew in his power with a greedy gulp. Only one, for fear of hurting him.

Hunter collapsed next to her, and she turned and wound herself around him. Drowsy from the exertion and almost drunk with pleasure, Phoebe found her limbs so weak it took too much effort to move. She didn't want Hunter to move either.

"Can we take a nap?" she asked.

He smiled, and she studied the mouth that had stoked her passion so generously. "If you like."

She forced herself to look up into his eyes, once again their normal deep gray with the blue ring. As she smoothed his hair back from his temple, a sweet wave of tenderness struck her. "How did you get to be so fearless?" she asked.

"Why would I be afraid of you, Phoebe? You sacrificed yourself for your sire, then for a sixteen-year-old girl. I knew you wouldn't go too far."

She supposed the question should be, who would sacrifice themselves for her? Who cared for her enough to do so?

Hunter had come the closest.

But would they have the time to discover what more they could have together? What more he wanted from her? She wanted him. Wanted to be his mate. But even with the blood and the power they had shared, she felt weak. "Thank you for all you've done for me, Hunter."

His gaze grew sharp, hawkish, making his features appear noble. "I'm not through yet, Phoebe. Not by a long shot. We're going to get Trevor, and he will pay for everything he has done. You're going to live, and we will have time to be together. As much time as we want."

She longed to believe him.

Chapter 12

HUNTER PACED THROUGH the house, his footsteps echoing in the empty rooms. There were two overstuffed couches and two chairs in the living room, a dining room table and chairs, bar stools at the island in the kitchen, and bedroom furniture in Phoebe's room in the basement, but the rest of the house remained empty.

The Hamilton brothers got up soon after he and Phoebe, and they also paced the house, anxious for some kind of action. A security team of fifty vampires was scattered throughout the area surrounding the house, waiting for Trevor to arrive. He wouldn't be alone, Hunter was certain.

The Bernard shifters, Babe, Shirley, and Marian prowled the house, watchful, on edge, and as impatient for this damnable waiting to end as he.

Hunter paused to look out the south window of the room Phoebe called her office.

"How is she?" Babe asked from his position at the west end.

Hunter fisted his hands. His voice, roughened with emotion, came out like gravel. "I encouraged her to sleep a little longer to conserve her strength. She won't live another twenty-four hours if they don't find an antidote."

"I heal pretty quick, probably not as fast as you, but almost. Would my blood help her?"

Hunter bit back the instinctive growl of denial. But he needed to tame his jealousy if he wanted to help Phoebe. He wanted no other male to feed her, but if the big shifter's blood could do her some good...

"We could try it, Babe. If Phoebe's open to it."

"When she first started coming up here and prowling at night, we thought she was hunting, so we trailed her for a couple of nights. She was stalker quiet and fast as lightning. We had a hard time keeping up with her. Then when she turned her camera on us, we realized the only things she was hunting were images. It didn't please us much, having our picture taken in full bear shift, especially since she'd managed to double back on us and ambush us with her camera.

"She invited us to a sit-down meal the next day at Arthur's house, so we could draw up some ground rules. She said she wanted to share the peace and quiet of our valley, and the only hunting she intended to do was with her camera."

Hunter swallowed. "What did she fix for you?"

"Best damn steak I've ever had, loaded baked potatoes, grilled asparagus, and homemade yeast rolls. And beer. She watched us eat every bite. She even fixed a fancy cheesecake, but we were too full to eat it, so she sent it home to my mom. We ate it later that night.

"She charmed the whole family, and convinced us she was sincere. She's the most human vampire I've ever met, and I've met quite a few at the store. But then she's not exactly a typical human, either."

"No, she's not." Hunter smiled. "Cheeseburgers. They were her favorite, and she still misses them."

"Must be rough living on a liquid diet, huh?"

"Sometimes. It's been too long for me to care. It's harder for her."

"Do you want to ask her about the blood, or should I?"

"I'll stay here on watch in your place while you go down and ask her." And it was better if he didn't watch another male feed her.

Babe paused at the office door. "She's not interested in any of us. We're like big brothers to her."

Damn, the big shifter was trying to ease his concerns. Surprised by Babe's sensitivity, Hunter glanced over his shoulder at him. "A good thing. Otherwise I'd have to kill you."

Babe's laughter followed him out into the hallway.

Phoebe was weakening rapidly, and he was getting desperate. He couldn't remember a time when this special blend of panic and fear churned in his gut, but it was happening now. Every muscle was tense with it. He couldn't lose her. He couldn't go through it with another mate. And she was his mate. He'd felt it from the moment they met.

He took out his phone and called Arthur again.

"They've got the antidote."

"You need to send it by someone, now. She's very weak, Arthur."

"I've contacted Zaira O'Shea and asked if she can teleport the cure to you the moment they arrive. Horatio should be here any moment."

Hunter braced his forearm against the window facing and stared out at the verdant landscape of grass, brush, and trees surrounding the house. The place was a nightmare to defend. There was too much cover.

But he wasn't going to worry about that until after Phoebe was taken care of. "Get her there now so she'll be waiting and ready."

"Immediately."

Hunter closed his eyes. He had to believe Zaira would make it in time.

"Is Ricci still there with you?"

"Yes, he is."

"Are you going to give him the antidote when it arrives?"

"Not until I know Phoebe has taken it first and is better."

"Good." Hunter knew it was vindictive, but it gave him some satisfaction knowing the master vampire would have to suffer a little longer. "I want the bastard to live and face the National Council. I contacted them yesterday, and they should be there in a few hours. They'll have some things they want to discuss with him."

"Good. I'll make certain he survives long enough to face them."

Twenty minutes later, Babe returned with Phoebe in tow. Her cheeks had a soft dusting of color, so he could tell she had fed. Jealousy gave him a hard punch, but he shoved it away. Whatever helped her survive until the antidote arrived.

She sauntered up next to him. Feeling possessive, he looped an arm around her waist and pulled her close. He caught her smile as she leaned into him.

"Feeling better?"

She nodded.

"It's nearly three, so the second security team Arthur was supposed to send should be here any time."

"We might be more help up on the widow's walk. We can see better at night than anyone else. And I'd like some fresh air."

Hunter took out his cell phone. "Babe, you have a cell phone?"

The big Shifter looked over his shoulder from his position at the window. "Dude, does a bear shit in the woods?"

Hunter laughed, and Phoebe's husky chuckled joined in.

"What's your number?" He keyed it in while Babe rattled it off. "We'll text when we see something."

✧   ✧   ✧

THE MOON GLOWED from behind a cloud as they stepped out onto the roof. Beneath the midnight blue, the sky had the purplish-pink look of a newly formed bruise as lightning too distant for the sound to carry flashed intermittently. The breeze brushing against her skin felt moist, promising rain, which would make it even harder to see an attack coming. The scent of pine and fresh greenery sharpened with each swirling gust.

She scanned the distant forest and tilted her head to listen. When Trevor came, he would be at his strongest. And he wouldn't be alone.

She would not hide below in her newly built panic room while everyone else was in danger. She had to fight. But she was getting weaker by the moment.

Phoebe assessed her physical condition while she followed the railing and looked out over the property. Babe's strong, healing blood gave her a boost, but she didn't know how long it would last. She was weaker already, her heart straining to beat now, and she felt unbelievably drained. Plus, the bite on her neck had turned green with infection. It had been nearly sixty years since she'd even seen anything like it.

She didn't want to die. Not now she'd found Hunter and she'd broken away from Arthur to have her own life. She beat back the panicked rise of emotion threatening to choke her.

"Will you tell me where you're from?" she asked, desperate for a distraction, desperate to know him, to spend time with him. But it was slipping away.

"I'm originally from Boston, but I've traveled all over the globe."

"You've been alive since the seventeen hundreds."

"Yes. As a young apprentice, I helped print the first regular newspaper in Boston, and made my living as a writer for the paper. After four years there, I moved on to New York and worked as a carpenter. It was there that I met Vlad, or rather he fell upon me and turned me. When I awoke, I ran as far from New York as I could get. I lived through earthquakes in San Francisco, tornados in Kansas, and floods in Pennsylvania. Vlad caught up with me in San Diego and convinced me to stop running and join him. By then I'd been a vampire for some time, and I decided I needed direction in my life and a stable home. I met Blythe while we worked cases for Vlad involving rogue vampires. He was already working to gain some kind of control over the clans and keep the carnage to a minimum."

"Is that even possible? The nature of the beast is to be as brutal as possible."

"Not for all of us, Phoebe."

She thought about how gentle, and tender he was. She looked away so he wouldn't see her tears. "He and Arthur have a lot in common."

"That could be why they stay in such close contact."

She wanted Hunter to know about her. To share something personal. As part of the Vampire Security Council, he would be required to testify against her, and tell them about what she could do. Did it really matter now?

She drew a deep breath. "My great-grandmother was a witch. A fire witch. Because GG—that's what we called her—married a human, and so did her children, our family considered ourselves human. We assumed her abilities died with her, and that none of us had inherited any special talents.

"When I turned nineteen, I had my first..." She hadn't felt embarrassed in a long time, and had to ease into saying the words. "My first sexual experience. Which didn't turn out exactly as I'd hoped. I won't go into it, but suffice it to say I was a little upset by the rat-bastard dick-with-ears. While we were arguing, his car caught on fire and exploded."

Hunter's bark of laughter made her smile. "I'm sorry." He laughed again. "No I'm not. I'm amazed that the men in your life are such—" He seemed to fish around for the right word.

"Losers?" Phoebe suggested. She'd been a bum magnet then, and it hadn't changed much after she became a vampire. But maybe her taste in men was improving—or her luck.

If she lived through the next few days, she hoped he

wouldn't walk away from her like every other man in her life. The look on his face after they made love gave her hope.

She fell silent when Hunter turned from surveying the distant treetops and tilted his head in a listening attitude. She added her own auditory powers and heard only the quiet rustle of the stiffening breeze.

"Go on, Phoebe," he urged.

"It wasn't until later, after several similar blazes cropped up, that I realized I was the one causing them. I didn't dare let myself get upset for fear I'd set the house on fire. I couldn't talk to my parents about it. They'd have been terrified, and I wanted to spare them the worry. So I went to see Zaira. That was before she opened her PI office, but I heard rumors about her. Luckily, she took one look at me and understood what was happening."

She leaned against the railing and scanned the area. "She helped me relax a little, and gave me some instruction on how to control things. Then she took me deep into the mountains and let me practice, so we could get an idea what I could do. It turns out I'm not a traditional witch. I tried to cast spells, but it never felt natural to me, and they always went a little sideways. Not a good thing if you're going to wield any kind of power that will boomerang back to you threefold."

She caught Hunter's quick grin and answered it with one of her own.

"Recently she suggested I go see several of her friends, more powerful than her. She thought they might be able to help. And they did."

"Not all witches and shifters are as open to the type of interaction you seem to inspire, Phoebe."

"Well, they were open to our meeting. But once they discovered I'm part vampire, part witch they were even more motivated to help me learn some new skills and hone several others. Mostly control."

"Did they teach you how to cloak yourself or others?"

She raised a brow.

"The Hamiltons appeared out of nowhere the first night we met."

She shrugged. "I couldn't do it consistently until after we worked together. By exercising my powers more, they changed, and I had to learn how to control them all over again. In some ways my skills have become more powerful, and in others more unpredictable."

"When you were attacked, Arthur sensed what you were and turned you."

Phoebe took a deep breath. "I'm sure it was a kind of experiment. I almost set him on fire when I first woke up. My fight or flight had gone to all fight. Had he been a hair slower, I'd have killed us both.

She moved her shoulders, uncomfortable with the memories. "It took a while for me to control my rage at being turned." Sometimes it still cropped up, though there was nothing short of death that could be done about it.

Only now she was facing death did she realize how much she wanted to live. She might be on the brink of having a real life with someone who really cared for her.

"Eventually Arthur earned my trust, and we became closer. Then he began to worry about how the Vampire Security Council would react if they learned what I can do."

"Vlad is the head of the Council, and he's already sensed what you can do, Phoebe. If he meant to end you, he would already have done it."

"I think he's waiting to see how things play out. If I don't survive, he will have saved himself the trouble."

From his stoic expression, she suspected Hunter had similar thoughts.

"He's always on the lookout for talented people. He might offer you a job."

She shook her head. "I'm not sure I could trust him enough to work for him. I'd be too busy looking over my shoulder."

"Do you trust me, Phoebe?"

She glanced over her shoulder at him. At the look in his eyes, her heart stumbled and shook. She'd made love with this male. He'd treated her with respect and concern since the beginning. But if it came down between a tug of war between her and his sire, his loyalty would have to remain with Vlad. She took a breath to say as much.

Hunter was a blur as he rushed forward and knocked her

off her feet. A blazing arrow streaked past, missing them by a fraction of an inch, and embedded itself in the log wall behind them.

"It seems they mean to fight fire with fire," he commented, his fingers flying while he texted Babe to warn the others.

Rage ignited her powers and determination. Trevor Ricci had taken all he was going to take from her. This was her home, and he wasn't going to damage it. She drew the fire to her, and the arrow sputtered and went out.

The two of them leapt to their feet and scanned the area around them. Beneath the cover of darkness and the heavy brush, the mountain was alive with hundreds of vampires slowly making their way toward the house. The sounds of fighting to the west reached them.

A text dinged on Hunter's phone. "You have to get downstairs, Phoebe. Zaira is here and has the antidote."

"There isn't time for that now, Hunter."

Another text came in. "The other security team has met with stiff resistance down the mountain, and they're fighting their way up here. I've forwarded the message to Babe."

Thunder sounded from the west, and lightning split the night sky like a knife. At the speed it traveled, the storm would be upon them within the next half hour.

A group of vampires reached the cleared area around the house, their faces moonlit as, one after another, they looked up and saw Hunter and Phoebe on the widow's walk.

Others were emerging from the woods.

Phoebe reached out, pulling energy from the elements around her, intending to encircle the house with a band of fire to keep them at bay. Fire erupted from the ground and followed the path she'd visualized. Most of them stumbled back in fear.

"They're going to jump," Hunter shouted. His fangs lengthened and he braced himself for battle.

A group of ten leapt up toward the widow's walk. Phoebe thrust her power at them. In mid-flight, the vampires' bodies burst into flames, turned to ash, and drifted down. The wind picked up, whipping the powder around until it descended like a cloud on the next group, dusting their dark clothes and making them far easier to see.

She braced a hand atop the railing when a wave of dizziness hit.

"How long can you keep this up?"

"As long as I have to." The release of power from the elements drained her, but she didn't have a choice. She had to shield the people who were here to protect her for as long as she could.

Without fuel to burn, the circle of fire began to peter out. At least fifty vampires milled around the perimeter of the yard, waiting for it to die.

"Would you text Zaira and tell her to ward the house so they can't get in?" she asked.

Hunter's fingers flew as he texted Babe again. "She's

already on it. We have to get inside right now, in fact, or we'll be locked out."

They rushed to the door. The invisible barrier knocked them both back. Two vampires landed on the widow's walk and raced toward Phoebe and Hunter with vampire speed. Hunter leapt into the air, crashed down on top of the taller of the two, and snapped his neck before flinging the body off the roof.

The other male came to a sliding halt and reached for Phoebe. "You don't look all that dangerous," he said with a smirk.

Before she could do anything, Hunter ripped his throat out. The vampire collapsed into a heap. He tossed aside the chunk of flesh and bent to wipe his hand on the dead male's shirt. "We need to get off this roof, Phoebe. Others will follow these two almost immediately."

"They're coming now. I'll cloak us until we jump clear."

Hunter caught her hand and they ran to the railing.

Ten vampires landed on the roof. Four of them rushed to the door, but bounced off it, as they had.

Several vampires leaped against the exterior of the house, systematically searching for a chink in Zaira's wards.

Hunter took her hand and looked at her. "Ready?"

"Yes."

They leaped over the railing together and landed a few feet from a group of seven. Two males ran forward, their heads whipping back and forth, searching the area.

Though she felt close to drained, Phoebe twirled her finger around and around, sending pain toward the small group. The two closest to them screamed and fell to the ground. The others soon followed.

"Let's go," Hunter urged.

They leapt once more, and landed at the edge of the clearing. The brush and tall grass tore at them while they ran deep into the woods with several vamps close behind them. Hunter jerked her behind a large tree and held her close. The group ran past them for several hundred feet, then came to a halt. Phoebe and Hunter remained where they were, unmoving.

"I don't know what it was, but it's gone now," one said as they walked past on their way back to the house.

As soon as they could no longer hear receding footsteps, Hunter urged her deeper into the forest.

Winded, Phoebe gasped, "Text Zaira, and tell her we're taking cover, and not to drop the wards for any reason."

"Done."

When he grabbed her hand again, she staggered against him. Keeping the cloak up had drained her more than she could believe. "Hunter...I think I'd better rest."

He caught her close. "Is there somewhere we can take shelter? It's going to rain any moment."

"There's a hunters' blind about two hundred yards north. It's like a box with holes cut out for windows. It was here when I bought the property, and I've been meaning to have the boys tear it down."

He bent and scooped her up.

Too spent to complain, Phoebe wound her arms around his neck and clung to him while he carried her.

"I loved making love with you this evening. I thought we'd have more time."

"We will, Phoebe."

She turned her face against his neck so he wouldn't see her tears.

"I've found the blind. Do you want to try climbing up into it?"

"Yes." Halfway up the rickety planks hammered into the tree, she had to rest. Her muscles quivered, and a strange, airless feeling weakened her further. But Hunter was right behind her to give her support and a boost when she had difficulty crawling up inside the wooden structure.

She lay curled on her side for several minutes, too weak to move. The floor, hard and rough, smelled of fresh wood. The flicker and flash of the lightning moved closer, and the thunder that followed rumbled loud enough to vibrate the floor beneath her cheek.

Hunter leaned over her. She struggled to see his face clearly. Her night vision was going.

"We have to get the antidote, Phoebe."

She rested a hand on his arm and felt the tension in his muscles.

"It's too dangerous. I don't think I could keep us cloaked

long enough to get inside. We'd be ripped to pieces before we ever made it. If they managed to get inside, they'd do the same to the others. We have to wait them out. Or until the others make it up the mountain."

"Phoebe…"

She knew what he was going to say. She might not have that much time. "Will you lie with me and hold me?"

He leaned back against the trunk of the tree and lifted her into his lap to hold her against him. "Don't let go, Phoebe."

Chapter 13

HUNTER SWALLOWED BACK a roar of frustration and anguish. Her power was waning, and had dulled to a flat warmth.

He reached for his phone and laid it on the floor to type in a text. He had never sent an SOS to Vlad in all the years he worked for him, but he did now. Once he finished, he put the phone away and adjusted the two of them so he could hold her closer.

"You have to hold on, Phoebe."

"I love it when it rains like this." She sounded drowsy.

The steady shower created a soft, trickling sound while the wind blew mist through the open windows to dampen their clothes.

Lightning flashed, and the thunderclap was so close it vibrated inside his chest. The storm seemed to have settled over them. The elemental fury outside made him edgy and ramped up his gnawing sense of panic.

"I want to go out and see if they've given up, Phoebe."

She remained silent so long he thought she might have gone to sleep.

"Please don't be long."

"I won't. I promise."

"I'll lie down for a while until you return." She eased away from him and curled upon the rough floor.

What if she died while he was gone? He couldn't bear the thought of her being alone.

He slid down to lie beside her and brushed her hair back from her face. "You have to stay strong long enough to give us a chance. I believe we can have something special, Phoebe." He bit his own wrist because he didn't think she was strong enough to do it. "Feed from me. It will give you strength." He placed his wrist against lips. She drank weakly from the bite, her eyes on his face.

She pushed aside his arm after taking only a few short drinks. "I love you, too, Hunter."

It had been more than a hundred years since he had wept, but he was close now. "Don't leave me. You have to fight."

"I'll try."

He kissed her and tasted his own blood on her lips. "I'll be right back."

She gave him a small, sleepy nod. "Be careful."

He scanned the forest for movement from all three windows before leaping to the ground through the hole cut in the bottom. Caution urged him to take his time.

A hundred yards through the forest he found twenty of Phoebe's security team members lying dead in a heap. He sped from tree to tree until he made it to the cleared area around the house. The dead littered the ground where a hand-to-hand battle had raged. But there were still at least twenty vampires milling around in front of the house, and two wandering around on the widow's walk, waiting for the protective wards to fall.

Trevor Ricci paced back and forth in front of the house. His shirt clung to him, rusty with blood, and the others were just as bloody. If Hunter could kill him, the rest of his clan would either die or give up. But could he reach Trevor before they realized what was happening?

He slipped back into the brush, pulled his phone out, and wiped it as dry as he could. At Babe's answer, he asked, "How many are left outside behind the house?"

"About twenty."

Three vampires, three Shifters, and one witch to take out forty vampires. But if he could kill Trevor, there might be none left—if Trevor had turned them all. Why would they fight for him otherwise?"

"I'm going to take Trevor out. Phoebe's dying, and she has to have that antidote right now."

"We'll be watching for when you make your move, and we'll help as much as we can."

Hunter looked to the east and saw a feeble glow. Sunrise would be in just under an hour, and he wouldn't be able to move Phoebe after that. It was now or never. He removed the gun at the small of his back, ejected the clip, checked it, then slapped it back in place. Fifteen rounds for thirty-five vampires.

He rose from his crouched position, ran his fingers through his dripping hair to comb it off his forehead, and embraced the sudden rush of adrenaline that hit his system.

If he died, Phoebe would die. That wasn't going to happen.

He focused on Trevor and ignored the rest of his minions when he stepped out of the forest and sauntered toward them. Perhaps because he was wearing a wet turtleneck, slacks, and windbreaker, no one seemed to notice him.

Trevor smirked when he stopped in front of him.

"Trevor Ricci?" Hunter asked, though he knew the answer already.

"Yeah."

Hunter removed his ID from his inner jacket pocket and flipped it open. "Hunter Knox. I represent the National Vampire Security Council. You're wanted for questioning in the death of Angelina Gomez in Texas and Andre Cassard in Louisiana, as well as the poisoning of Armanno Ricci and several members of his household, the death of your human servant, Jeb, and the poisoning of your wife, Phoebe Stewart."

"You don't say. Are you the only one they sent?" He smirked again.

"Yes. I'm the only one they could spare at the moment. I need you to come with me."

Trevor threw his head back and laughed. "I'm a little busy right now. So, no, I don't think I will." His features went taut with aggression while he glanced past Hunter to the vampires poised to attack. Hunter felt them closing in. "Kill—"

With lightning speed, Hunter pulled the gun at the small of his back and emptied the clip into Trevor's chest. Trevor stumbled back and fell, his expression stunned.

Hunter leaped forward, thrust his hand into the other vampire's chest, and ripped out his heart.

Time stood still for one second, then two. More than half the vampires standing in the front yard crumpled and died with the suddenness of their sire. The others looked around, and seeing the numbers of their dead comrades, broke and ran.

The front door to the house burst open, and the Hamilton brothers roared out in pursuit. Sounds of fighting came from the back. A roar and several screams split the air.

In the distance, the whomp-whomp-whomp of a helicopter flying close by echoed in the valley.

Hunter rushed into the house, yelling for Zaira.

She appeared beside him instantly. "I'm here. Where is she?"

"A hunters' blind back in the forest to the north. Do you have the antidote?"

Zaria patted her sweater pocket.

Hunter picked her up and ran full out. She left him

standing at the base of the tree as she zapped herself up into the blind. He climbed the wooden strips slowly, afraid of what he might find.

Even if it worked, the sun was coming, and they wouldn't know whether the antidote worked for hours, because Phoebe always died at the first hint of sunrise.

Zaira was chanting a spell when he entered the blind. Her eyes were closed, her features intent. After several moments, she stopped. Tears streaked down her cheeks. "The spell is to push the antidote through her system more quickly. I'm sorry I put the wards up too soon."

Hunter knelt next to Phoebe and clasped her hand in both of his. "It was what Phoebe wanted. She didn't want anyone hurt on her behalf. She knew there were hundreds against the nine of us, and the security forces were killed before they reach us."

Phoebe's hand was cold, but was it the chill of death or sleep? He searched for the small spark of power he'd felt before he left...and found nothing. He rested his forehead against his knee and averted his face while the pain ripped through him.

He brought her hand to his mouth and brushed his lips back and forth against her skin. All the possibilities they had lost rose up to torment him. The way she looked when she stepped into the tub before they made love. Her glow of complete contentment afterward.

A familiar head and shoulders popped through the hole

in the floor. "Are you going to get the hell out of my way so I can do something about this, or are you going to continue to grieve?" Vlad snapped while he climbed the rest of the way into the blind, the hum of his power as powerful as a jet engine.

"Do you still have the hypodermic you used to inject her?"

Zaira, wide-eyed with fear, handed him the syringe.

He shoved back the sleeve of his turtleneck sweater, removed the cap, and jabbed the needle into his forearm, withdrawing an entire syringe of blood. He knelt beside Phoebe. "She's truly dead, but since it just happened, there may yet be hope." He injected the blood directly into a vein in her arm, went through the process four more times, then put the cap back on the syringe and stuck it in his pocket.

"I'll take her to the house," Zaira said, tears still wet on her cheeks.

Hunter nodded, unable to speak.

She and Phoebe were gone in the blink of an eye.

Hunter rose from his crouched position and turned to face his sire. "Is there truly hope?"

"Yes. But what she was when she died this time may not be what she is when she awakens."

Shock held Hunter immobile for several moments. "What do you mean?"

"I am the oldest living vampire on earth, Hunter. When I changed you, you only sipped my blood. I've just injected

Phoebe four times. When she awakens, there may be changes in what she can do and what she might be."

"You mean she may no longer be the Phoebe we know?" And love.

"Possibly not."

The words hit him like a sledgehammer, but then he shook his head determination, beating back his anxiety. As long as she was alive, they could deal with the rest of it together.

DAWN BROKE, AND as the sun rose, the dead caught fire and burned. Babe and his brothers called in help to ensure the small blazes didn't set the whole mountainside alight. A drenching rain helped, but left behind ugly, blackened heaps of ash surrounding the house. Hunter wielded a shovel along with Babe and his brothers, while they labored together to scoop up the remains and bury them deep in the forest.

Every half hour he returned to Phoebe's bedroom. Zaira sat next to the bed waiting for some sign of life, and promised to text him if there was any change.

Around noon a text came in. Hope surged, and he dropped the shovel and jerked his phone free. It was Vlad. Armanno Ricci had been given the antidote and was expected to live. He had been sentenced to five hundred years in solitary confinement. It was the only way to punish him without killing the many vampires he had created, and it meant he would lose his place in his clan for five hundred years.

Ricci deserved to die because of what he and his son did to Phoebe, for what they did to all the others, for all the lives they caused to be ended here, in this place.

The storm of rage and pain left him feeling hollow, leaving behind a hovering grief, waiting to consume him if Phoebe truly died.

By midday he had to take his rest. It had been years since he was still up so long after sunrise. He slipped into Phoebe's room.

Zaira rose from her chair. "I was just going to text you. Look! I took the bandage off her throat, and her wounds are healed."

In two strides he was beside the bed and to gently turn Phoebe's head and study her neck. The puncture wounds had vanished without a trace, as had the horrible bruise and infection. Relief diminished some of his worry.

Pheobe wouldn't rise until sunset or a little after. He just had to hold on to the hope she would be the same woman he fell in love with. "I'll stay with her. Why don't you go home for a while?" It might not be good to have anyone non-vampire here when Phoebe awoke. What if she had reverted to her newly turned vamp state? With Vlad's blood, anything was possible.

Zaira searched his face, the skin below her eyes smudged

with exhaustion.

"I'll text you if anything happens," he added.

She looked away. "I'm sorry, Hunter."

"It wasn't your fault. It was Ricci and his bastard son's. They're responsible for everything."

She nodded, and in the next heartbeat she was gone.

Hunter took a shower and dressed in sleep pants and a T-shirt. Then he lay beside Phoebe and studied her face for several minutes. He covered her hand with his and reached out through the connection, seeking some sign her power was returning. When he discovered a tiny spark buried deep inside her, he concentrated on fanning it with his own power. It seemed to grow for a moment, then died back down.

She would fight her way back. He knew she would. It would just take time.

Chapter 14

P HOEBE WOKE AT the first hint of sunset. She lay quietly
for several minutes, trying to orient herself. Her mind
felt dull and slow, as though she'd been asleep for eons.

She turned over to find a male sleeping beside her wearing flannel sleep pants and a T-shirt. She studied him,
deciding there was something familiar about him, but, no
matter how she cudgeled her memory, she couldn't figure
out how she knew him, or who he was.

He had a very masculine, compelling face, though, all
planes and angles, except for his mouth. It was exceptional.
Just looking at it made her want to taste him. The quick rush
of arousal caught her unaware, and she gasped. Why was
she feeling like this when she had just laid eyes on him?

She slipped free of the bed and backed away from it,
studying the room. It, too, seemed familiar, but it obviously
hadn't been lived in very long. It was too barren of personal
things, and too clean. Was it a rented room? And why was
she here with a strange male?

Careful not to wake the sleeping vampire, she wandered
to the door. She turned the knob to open it, but it was

locked. She studied the electronic panel next to the door with its buttons, but she couldn't think which to push, or what order to key them in.

Why would she be locked in? Was it to keep her in, or others out?

The rustle of the sheets behind her triggered sudden anxiety and she jerked around to face the bed.

"How do you feel, Phoebe?"

His voice sounded familiar, too. Husky, deep, and dark like the male. His rich brown hair, medium length, lay in heavy layers against his head. His gray eyes studied her with worry and concern.

"I'm well. Who are you?"

He flinched, then stiffened, as though the question hurt him. "My name is Hunter. Hunter Knox."

"Hunter." She murmured his name, feeling the texture of it in her mouth. His face was so arresting, his gaze so intense, they triggered that rush of desire again, as though her body hungered for him while the momentous reason she responded to him flirted around the edges of her memory.

"Why are we here in this locked room?"

"This is your room, in your house. You've been ill. It's locked, just as a precaution, because we've been under attack."

He was lying. "I can't be ill. I'm a vampire."

"You were poisoned, Phoebe."

The word poison sent a shard of fear through her, sharp

as a stake. Her hand went to her throat. "But I'm better now?"

"Yes. We were able to give you the antidote, and my sire shared his blood with you. You were—near death. I believe it's why you're confused."

Confused didn't even begin to cover what she was thinking and feeling.

"Why are you with me here?"

She read pain on his face before he replied. "We have been together for a short while."

So the feelings she was experiencing were real. Relief settled some of her panic.

He rose, moved to the door, punched in the code, and opened it. "You may want to dress. There are others in the house."

She looked down at her nightshirt and bare feet.

With the door standing open, her anxiety eased.

A compulsion to touch him arrested her and she clenched her hand at her side to control it.

"Who else is here?"

"Your bodyguards, the Hamilton brothers, and the Bernards, Gabe, Marion, and Shirley."

Her tension evaporated when she remembered who he was talking about. She ran her fingers through her hair. "I need you to tell me everything that's happened."

"What is the last thing you remember?"

She closed her eyes and strained to pinpoint the last

event. "The wedding. Please tell me I didn't marry that narcissistic, blood-sucking douchebag."

"You did. He poisoned you at the wedding."

She caught her breath as outrage stormed through her. "That asshole! I'll kill him."

"You don't have to worry about him anymore."

The flat, ruthless expression on his face held her silent. Instead of frightening her, it gave her a tingling thrill.

Without thinking, she touched his arm. "I'm getting dressed. Then you can explain everything."

By the time she finished her shower, the grogginess she awakened with had passed. As she wrapped a towel around her hair, her attention snagged on the tub. She caught a quick flash of Hunter, his skin gleaming with soap, the muscles beneath his skin lovingly traced by the water while she rinsed the foam away. Her heart thundered. The intimacy between them had given her more than pleasure.

She needed to hear all the details. She needed to know how Hunter felt about her. And she needed to know how he had changed her long-standing aversion to romance.

She dressed and brushed her teeth and hair, emerging from the bathroom to find him wearing dark slacks and a pullover knit shirt that delineated his broad shoulders and the musculature of his chest and stomach.

She understood why she was so drawn to him. It was the dangerous, bad-boy aura about him. His eyes...glowing blue as he leaned over her... The memory caught at her heart and made it hammer against her ribs. She placed a hand over it. It had not beat like that in decades.

"Do you want to feed?" he asked.

Maybe she should. Maybe it would help her remember. "Yes."

He removed two packages of blood from the small re- frigerator and handed her one. She sat down on the end of the bed. "This room seems familiar, and you seem familiar."

The relief in his expression was hard to acknowledge. What if she never remembered what they had felt for each other? He would be hurt. She couldn't allow him to be hurt.

He sat beside her while they finished the meal and talked about the house and her plans to live here. "I'm afraid your landscaping was destroyed during the confrontation with Trevor's clan. The Bernards and I tried to clean up, but there are areas of burned grass and ash coating everything, and the smell is lingering."

"Why can't I remember any of this?"

"We were attacked, and Zaira warded the house to pre- vent them from being able to enter or destroy it. You and I had to take cover in a hunting blind north of here, so we didn't witness much of the battle. After you and I repelled the initial attack, you became too weak to fight."

She didn't feel weak now. She felt she could lift the house if she needed to. She sucked down the last of the blood in the bag and tossed the empty plastic in a small trashcan, then beckoned Hunter to follow her.

On the way upstairs, she curled her fingers around his arm, her sense of familiarity with him increasing.

They entered the kitchen. As soon as they saw her, the Hamilton brothers, all big, broad, and wooly with their curly hair and beards, greeted her with a fist bump and a hug. The oldest asked, "How do you feel?"

"Good. Strong."

"I can say this now it didn't happen. We didn't think you were going to make it, Phoebe. So glad you're back."

"Thank you."

They left the brothers to finish their evening meal and went outside.

"I was really ill." It was more a statement than a question.

Hunter cupped his hand over hers on his arm. "You were dying, Phoebe."

She found that bit of information too unsettling to dwell on.

They settled on the porch steps under the soft light of the moon, and he explained everything...except when and how they were intimate. She knew they had been. Her body responded to his nearness, to the sound of his voice, and the way he looked at her, with a rising need. She had never experienced anything quite like it.

She turned her attention on the surrounding yard to distract herself from her raging libido. It had been trampled, burned, and the plants and bushes she selected so painstakingly, destroyed. The signs of a tremendous battle were easy to read. Every time she drew in a breath, or when she spoke, she could taste the ashes of death and smell them.

She wished she could heal the earth as easily as she could burn it. She walked out into the yard and turned to face the house. The three-quarter moon looked as bright as a spotlight. She smelled bear. Were the Bernard brothers back from hunting? She scanned the nearby forest, but didn't see or hear them.

Perhaps if she warmed the air it would blow the stench away. She stretched out a hand and let just a hint of power ease out. A breeze rustled the trees and whipped along the ground, kicking up the ash.

She wiggled her fingers, spinning the breeze, much as she did with her fire sometimes, until the breeze became a dust devil of sorts, but made of ashes. She guided it along the ground, urging it from one spot to another, while it picked up the remnants of the battle and carried them away, over the distant hills to stretch out like a cloud of smoke, dissipate, and disappear.

"Could you do that before?" Hunter asked.

She thought about it. "Not exactly, and not with as much control."

"My sire warned me you might notice some differences in your powers."

Like the steady beat of her heart? "Who is your sire?"

"His name is Vlad Tepes."

"He can't be. He's been dead for six hundred years."

Hunter chuckled. "That's what you said the first time I told you."

Why couldn't she remember that? But an image invaded her mind of a vampire, tall, slim, with dark, intense eyes and a mustache. He stood in the kitchen with Hunter while she talked on her cell phone. His interest and his power... She'd been almost paralyzed with fear. She shivered just thinking about it. His blood ran through her body now? What would she owe him for such a sacrifice? Would he now be her sire? The thought sent her stomach tumbling.

She looked up to find Hunter watching her, naked hope in his eyes. It hit her with the force of a punch.

His phone rang, and he pulled it out and answered. "Yes." His gaze leapt to her face. "Now?" He stepped away to finish the call.

When he returned to her he was scowling.

"What is it?"

"I have to leave and go to Ricci's territory. His arrest and Trevor's death have thrown the clan into chaos. I have been elected to go there and take care of things before someone else moves in and attempts a takeover."

He paused, studying her closely, before adding, "Your name is still on the contract, Phoebe. You're legally Ricci's heir."

She shook her head. "He didn't really expect me to take over. And his people won't, either. I'd be walking into hostile territory." But he'd be in the same position, without anyone to back him up. The idea cramped her stomach with fear.

She didn't want him to leave. What would she do once he was gone? She had to remember. "Will you take me to the hunting blind?"

He clasped her hand and led the way.

The wooden box with its square-cut windows seemed a flimsy shelter. "It stormed last night. It may be wet inside," he warned.

She climbed up into the cramped space and backed against the tree trunk to make room for him. "I remember this being here when I bought the property."

An odd, quick sound like a woodpecker tapping at a hollow stump rattled in the distance. Hunter cocked his head and listened. "Vlad has sent a helicopter for me."

Not yet. She wasn't ready for him to go. Not yet.

Hunter's features were stiff, and his eyes kept straying to the floor at her feet. "You were dying, Phoebe. I had to leave you to get the antidote."

She saw the pain break through his composure, triggering an answering pain inside her.

She'd been cold when vampires weren't supposed to notice the change in temperature. She'd willed her heart to beat for him when it had wanted to stop...but it hadn't been enough. He asked her not to leave him.

"But you came back," she said. "I'm alive because you

came back."

His eyes took on the blue glow of powerful emotion held in check. The sound of the helicopter grew louder and louder. "I have to go." He stood abruptly, his hands fisted at his sides and his throat working as he swallowed. When he moved toward the opening in the floor, she caught his arm.

He caressed her fingers with his own, his voice huskier when he gazed in her eyes and told her, "I'll wait as long as it takes for you to remember how much I love you, Phoebe."

Quick tears stung her eyes and ran down her cheeks. She reached for him and was suddenly in his arms, being held tight, his lean, muscular body aligned with hers like a perfectly fitted puzzle piece. He'd protected her, fed her, made love to her, saved her. She fought to stay alive for him. For them.

"I remember, Hunter. It's all a jumble. But I remember." He kissed her, a desperate longing in the contact that fed them both. "You didn't leave me, you were here the whole time." She placed his hand over her steadily beating heart.

"I don't want to leave you behind. We can do this together."

"I don't know what my powers are like, Hunter."

"It'll be okay."

His reassurance made it easy. "Okay."

He stepped through the opening in the floor of the blind and dropped to the ground, moving aside to wait for her.

They walked toward the sound of the helicopter, but she

stopped and turned back. She dragged in power from the elements and, with a flick of her wrist, threw it toward the blind. The structure exploded into tiny, toothpick-sized pieces and powdered the forest floor.

She met Hunter's raised-eyebrow look.

She laughed. "That felt good."

His grin was all bad-boy vampire, sexy and suggestive. She'd seen that look before.

"I still can't read your mind, Hunter," she murmured against his ear. "But when I get on board the helicopter, I might just have to wiggle in my seat."

He chuckled the masculine sound erotic. "Be careful not to set your panties on fire, Phoebe."

THE END

If you liked this book and would like to continue the series here is the link to the next book:

BOOK 3 OF THE HAVE WAND, WILL TRAVEL SERIES
ADVENTURES OF A WITCHY WALLFLOWER

After 50 years of teaching magic-challenged witches, Madeline's found the perfect male witch to share a different kind of magic in her life. But his curse has another idea....

For fifty years Madeline Montgomery has taught magic-challenged witches how to cast spells. And she's good at it. When she loses her job at the college, she's thrown into an identity crisis. If she can't teach what will she do?

Broke and desperate, Jake Cunningham has borrowed money from the wrong witches. With a moniker like Jake The Rake floating around, he hasn't a chance of finding his next mark. Until he's made an offer he can't refuse—meet Madeline and he'll be a hundred thousand dollars richer.

When Jake shows up on Madeline's doorstep asking for her help, it's a goddess-send. While she teaches him to spell, he brings a different kind of magic into her life. For the first time she wants to throw caution to the wind and let her heart lead the way. But Jake insists he has a curse and if she gets too close she'll end up hating him.

But she's an expert at magic and a curse can be broken. Or can it?

FOR MORE INFORMATION ABOUT TERESA REASOR

Website:www.teresareasor.com

MILITARY ROMANTIC SUSPENSE
BREAKING FREE (Book 1 of the SEAL Team Heartbreakers)
BREAKING THROUGH (Book 2 of the SEAL Team Heartbreakers)
BREAKING AWAY (Book 3 of the SEAL Team Heartbreakers)
BREAKING TIES (A SEAL Team Heartbreakers Novella)
BUILDING TIES (Book 4 of the SEAL Team Heartbreakers)
BREAKING BOUNDARIES (Book 5 of the SEAL Team Heartbreakers)
BREAKING OUT (BOOK 6 of the SEAL Team Heartbreakers)
BREAKING POINT (A SEAL Team Heartbreakers Novella)
BREAKING HEARTS (Book 7 of the SEAL Team Heartbreakers)

SEALS IN PARADISE SERIES
HOT SEALS, RUSTY NAIL

PARANORMAL ROMANCE
TIMELESS
DEEP WITHIN THE SHADOWS (Book 1 of the Superstition Series)
DEEP WITHIN THE STONE (Book 2 of the Superstition Series)
WHISPER IN MY EAR
HAVE WAND, WILL TRAVEL (Book 1)
HAVE WAND, WILL TRAVEL: ONCE BITTEN, TWICE SHY (Book 2)
*HAVE WAND, WILL TRAVEL: ADVENTURES OF A WITCHY
WALLFLOWER (Book 3)*

HISTORICAL ROMANCE
CAPTIVE HEARTS
HIGHLAND MOONLIGHT
TO CAPTURE A HIGHLANDER'S HEART: THE TRILOGY

The Highland Moonlight Spinoff Trilogy in parts
TO CAPTURE A HIGHLANDER'S HEART: THE BEGINNING
TO CAPTURE A HIGHLANDER'S HEART: THE COURTSHIP
TO CAPTURE A HIGHLANDER'S HEART: THE WEDDING NIGHT

SHORT STORIES
AN AUTOMATED DEATH: A STEAMPUNK SHORT STORY
CAUGHT IN THE ACT: A HUMOROUS SHORT STORY

CHILDREN'S BOOK
WILLY C. SPARKS, THE DRAGON WHO LOST HIS FIRE

12481342R00118